Hope you enjoy! :)

The Cursed and Damned: The Daniels Family

By: Glenn Clay

The Cursed and Damned: The Daniels Family

This book is a work of fiction. Names, places, characters, and incidents are the product of the author's imagination. Any resemblance to actual persons, living or dead, business establishments, events, or locations is entirely coincidental.

Liza Cyrus, Editor

Printed in the United States of America

To my niece Sarah-for helping me stay creative. Also to Don Wildman, who has always told me to never give up.

Acknowledgements

First, I have to thank my editor and sister, Liza Cyrus. Without her, this book wouldn't be where it is today. Also, I would like to thank my parents and my brother for always believing in me and giving me time to follow my dreams. Without my whole family's support, I wouldn't have been able to finish this story.

I also want to thank Adam Gontier for inspiring me with his music that helped me continue writing this book. And I thank Jason Mraz for helping to inspire me to become more grateful for what I have, and also helping me live a greener life. I also owe a debt of gratitude to the suppliers of the caffeine I had to ingest to keep me awake those long nights of writing.

And last but certainly not least, I have to thank you the reader of this book. Without you, I wouldn't have had a reason to write. Thanks!

Chapter One

Early 20th Century

The red brick house sat on a large hill, overlooking the cemetery. A horse and buggy pulled up in front of the house and the back door swung open. Out stepped a tall, slender man with a long, black winter coat. He collected his bags and walked towards the house – his family home. As he approached the door, it was opened by unseen hands, and he walked in.

He looked up and his childhood memories came flooding back. It had been years since he had been home and he couldn't be happier to be there now. The door shut behind him. The maid came toward him holding up her hands as if she were going to take his belongings, instead she wrapped her arms around him.

"Mr. Daniels, it is so nice to see you. It has been years," she said as she embraced him tighter.

"It's nice to see you again, Judy," he said, wrapping his arms around her.

"What's the special occasion," she asked, pulling back from him.

"I guess I was a bit homesick, and figured I would come back for the fall festival this year. Oh, and Judy, you don't have to call me Mr. Daniels anymore, you can call me Evan," he said, looking down at her.

"I'm sorry. I guess old habits are hard to break." She said, as she picked up his luggage and started up the stairs.

"I can take those, Judy."

"No, that's ok, you should go see your parents…they're in the den," she said, turning back toward the stairs.

Evan walked into the den, as he came further into the room, he saw his mother sitting in the arm chair, facing the wall opposite him. He quietly walked up behind her and put his hands over her eyes.

"Guess who," he said. His mother jumped.

"Evan," she said joyfully.

"Yes! Where's father?"

"He's in the shed out back, tinkering with his inventions again," she said while rolling her eyes. Evan walked around to the chair opposite her. "What are you doing here? Not that I don't want you here, mind you, but it's such a surprise."

"Well, that was the point. I just I thought I would come to visit you and father. Are you and father going to the fall festival tonight," he asked, slightly tilting his head.

"No, we haven't been there in years. I guess we are just getting too old for silly things like festivals," she said, sipping from her tea cup. "Are you going?"

"Yes. I'm hoping to run into some old friends and maybe get myself a bite to eat," he said as he got up, "Can I get you or father anything while I am there?"

"No thank you dear, we'll have something here," she said, following him with her eyes.

"Ok, I will be back soon then," Evan said as he walked toward the front entrance.

He walked out the front door and stopped on the porch, closing his coat tighter around him as the fall winds picked up a bit. From the corner of his eye, he saw a man exit the cemetery. He decided to wait until the man passed before he walked up town. When the man drew closer, he saw his face was very pale and his eyes were piercing black. The man didn't seem to notice Evan standing on the porch and just kept walking towards the festival.

Evan walked off the porch and followed the stranger into the town. As they made their way downtown, he continued to keep close to the man. He couldn't help but think that this man might be up to something, given his odd behavior. The man turned and walked down an ally. Evan stopped at the ally entrance and watched the man continue walking. The man abruptly stopped, turned and stared right at him. The cold stare was enough to send chills down his spine, causing him to let out a slight gasp. Without hesitation, he left the man and began walking around the festival instead.

As he walked around town, he ran into several friends from his school days. Evan enjoyed reminiscing about days gone by. In fact all of it – the sights, sounds, smells – took him back to those days. The days of spending time trying to win useless toys, eating the fresh pie and drinking warm cider from the local bakery, walking the streets with friends, laughing and teasing each other. Once he had his fill of the festival, he got something to eat and was about to leave when he heard a blood curdling scream.

A girl came running out of the ally, holding onto her neck as blood was spurting over her fingers. She collapsed on the ground as everybody watched in horror. Then out came the strange man. The man wiped blood from his chin and looked around at everybody standing there. In an instant the crowd dispersed – screaming and running in different directions.

Evan, stumbling through the crowd, came upon the game booth row. He looked around for something to help slow down the man, but saw nothing. Then he spotted the gun shooting game. He ran over to it, pushing people out of the way. When he reached it, he loaded one of the guns and turned around to see where the man was. He knew that the gun may not stop the man, but it would at least slow him down. He spotted the man and started firing away as he ran towards him. The man fell to his knees and the woman he had attacked ran away screaming.

Evan ran over toward the man but in an instant, he was gone. He looked up and saw the man standing on top of one of the buildings. He then realized what he was dealing with. This was no man. He briefly looked down at the crowd, and when he looked back at the building, the man was gone. He turned and saw the figure right behind him, before he could run the vampire bit into his neck sending pain all through his body. Evan grabbed the creatures head and flipped him over his body, making the man hit the pavement with a thud. He stuck the gun to the man chest and sent a pellet into his heart.

He grabbed the man's body, tossed him over his shoulder and tried to decide where to take him. He remembered a construction site he had passed by and he decided to take the man there. When Evan got to the site he laid the body down on a stone and went to look for some rope to tie the man up with. As he came back to where he had left the body, he was shocked to find the man gone. Looking around the whole site there was no signs of the man's body. Evan was completely confused by this but then remembered this was no regular man he was dealing with. As he realized this, a searing pain went through his neck where he was bit. He made his way back into the town that was now quiet.

He stumbled into an ally and waited for death to come. He collapsed and was hidden behind a dumpster when it seemed his life was slipping away. He took one more deep breath and slumped back down as his eyes closed. Evan's body lay there in the ally for several hours, being passed by ladies of the night and men trying to make shady deals. Then, after the midnight hour, his eyes shot open revealing blood-shot eyes. His body began to twitch and convulse as if having a bad reaction to medication. His muscles tensed up and finally, with one last twitch his body, slumped back against the building that sat behind him. Evan stood up, confused, but started to make his way home.

He was trying to make sense of everything and keep control of himself, though an insatiable hunger was making it difficult. Keeping to the shadows, he grew anxious, when he looked up and saw his family's mansion rising from the hill above.

Evan's father was still in the shed working with his inventions when he heard a noise right outside the door. Thinking it was just one of the dogs or cats he went back to his work. Then he heard another sound and thought he should investigate – though it was the time of year for youngsters to wreak havoc near the graveyard. He walked out the door with a lantern in his hand looking around the yard. All of a sudden a dark shadow whipped past him and he lost his balance, almost toppling over. He balanced himself and turned to go back in the shed. Evan flew out of the shadows, grabbed his father by the neck, cracked it to one side and started to drain the blood out of his father. After he was done, he let go of his father, watching him slide down the exterior of the shed – eyes still open with a look of horror permanently fixed upon his face. His eyes still red with hunger, he proceeded to the house. He slowly opened the back door and looked around for the maid. He saw her headed towards the front of the house and lunged towards her. Within seconds he drained her of her blood as well. He then turned, seeking his mother. He ran into the den where his mother sat sleeping in the chair. He snuck up behind her, snapped her neck to one side and proceeded to drink her blood before she even had a chance to fully awaken. All of his family members were now dead and he could not have helped it. Then, with his hunger now fully satisfied, he began to realize what he had done. He fell to the floor, shaking and sobbing uncontrollably.

Once he gained control of himself, he knew that he could not continue to kill others for his own need – but he knew that the hunger was far too strong to control. He decided he would lock himself in the family crypt located under his parents' house until he could control his curse. He opened up the cellar door and descended into the dark. He walked towards the old rusted steel door of the crypt, opened it up and stepped inside. He made sure that the door could never be opened from the outside. He turned and took a seat in the corner reflecting on what had just happened. As he sat there, a rat ran over his foot. He decided that he would control himself by feeding on only rodents and other small animals that he could get his hands on. But first, he had to let everything die down before he could resurface.

Chapter Two

The Daniels estate had fallen silent for three years after the bodies of the Daniels family were found. Ivy had started inching up the side of the house, completely masking the front entrance and the bay window that was located in the front. Many rumors had been making their way around – that the house was haunted and monsters lived within its walls- but most people thought the rumors to be utter nonsense, and considered the house a sad reminder of those tragic deaths.

The murders that happened during the fall festival and the murders of the Daniels family had sent the town into a witch-hunt looking for the killer. But what the town didn't know was that the killer had been dead. It was Evan Daniels who had killed his family, though it was not entirely his fault. The original killer had turned him into a creature like himself. Evan Daniels was now a vampire, living in the family crypt in the cellar of his family's estate…hiding from the world and trying to gain control of his curse.

After three years of trying to control his rage and hunger, Evan knew he could resurface and act as a normal human being. He unlocked the crypt and slowly walked up the stairs to the cellar door. When he opened the door, a musky smell of dust and dried blood hit him in the face. He kept his hunger under control as he lit a candle and walked through the house. The blood stains were still on the floor where the maid had collapsed, and his mother's tea cup remained in the den where he had so savagely attacked her.

He sat the candle down and started to dust objects in the house. It was like time had stood still for three years. He continued cleaning through the night, moving from room to room with his single, lit candle. However, his movement in the house did not go unnoticed by the people who lived just down the hill.

A group of neighbors had gathered at the bottom of the hill, watching the house as the shadows within danced around the walls. This refueled the rumors of the past, and this made the neighbors fearful and anxious again. The candlelight eventually went out and briefly they relaxed. But still, they didn't know what or who had been in the house.

Evan, still confused and in shock from the events three years before, found he still had many things to learn about his curse. He soon came to find that most legends about vampires were untrue. He could touch a cross and not burn, and he could hold garlic cloves in his hands without turning his nose away. He could even go out in the sunlight without turning to dust-something he tested with much hesitation. At least this meant he could appear quite normal to others, and knowing this brought him some peace.

The cloud-filled sky showed the signs of fall coming into the town. He went out to the shed, grabbed a few landscaping tools and went into the front lawn. He proceeded to clean away the vines and weeds that had overtaken the house. He was so busy taking care of the landscaping, that he didn't hear the neighbor walking through the front gate at the bottom of the hill. Then he heard the gate creak and snapped his head towards its direction, seeing the neighbor heading up the steps.

He stopped trimming the bushes and met the neighbor halfway. He extended his hand out, as did the neighbor.

"Hello neighbor, are you new to town," the neighbor asked as he looked up at the decrepit house.

“No, actually I have been around here before visiting family,” Evan said as he watched the neighbor’s eyes, trying to gage his neighbor’s reactions to his responses.

“Oh? What’s your name?”

“Evan Daniels,” he said, instantly seeing the shock in the neighbor’s eyes.

“Daniels? You’re their son…I thought you were dead as well,” he said, looking baffled.

“No, I am a cousin. I shared my name with their son,” he said, trying to come up with a quick answer, “Yes, I inherited this house. I’m sorry, but I really need to get back to work if you don’t mind. Perhaps we can have the chance to sit down and get to know each other later?”

“Oh, absolutely, it looks like you have your work cut out for you. I will leave you at it. See you again soon,” he said as he waved, walking back towards the gate.

Evan returned to work pondering what he just told the neighbor. He hadn’t thought that he would have to explain himself, but he pulled it off. He just hoped that no more neighbors would bother him or make any further inquiries into his life or past.

After Evan had cleaned up the yard, he stood back and looked at his work. It still wasn't in the best of shape but it was better than it had been. The red brick building had a gothic elegance about it – made even more mysterious by its recent history. The mere size of the estate itself was incredible. Evan had never truly appreciated the beauty of the house he had grown up in, but he did now. As he admired it, he turned and looked down the hill at the town below. A smile crept over his face as he came to realize that this was going to be a new start for him.

He walked back to the house and shut the door behind him, getting prepared to rest a while and do more work within the house. As he sat in the den drinking a warm cup of blood from an unlucky cat, he heard a knock at the door. He jumped up, then slowly walked toward the door. Approaching the door, he could see someone running out the front gate. He quickly pulled open the door to see who it was, but couldn't see their face as they ran down the street.

He looked down and saw a package with his name written on it. Timidly he picked it up and brought it inside. He didn't understand – he knew nobody other than the neighbor he had just introduced himself to earlier. He opened the package up and saw newspaper clippings from that fateful night three years ago. He read through them, remembering the horror of that night, and saw a letter underneath all of the clippings. As he read it, shock and anger grew inside him. His mind started to race with thoughts. He had been found out, after only resurfacing for a day. He knew what he had to do. He could not risk this information spreading through town…he had to protect himself.

Chapter Three

Evan had only resurfaced for a day and had already made an enemy. He didn't know who was blackmailing him, but he knew he had to find out before it leaked to the community. He had to figure out where to start looking. It wasn't long before he got a clue.

There was a knock at the door. It was the neighbor he had met earlier that day, holding a copy of the day's paper.

"Just wanted to warn you, the newspapers are saying there's a killer lurking around town again," he said as he pointed toward the paper in his hand. "They think it's another vampire killing like three years ago."

"Really? How many have they killed so far," Evan asked as he looked closer at the paper.

"They say five so far - all at local cemeteries."

"Interesting," Evan said as he looked back up at the neighbor.

"Let's just hope it all dies down here soon," the neighbor said rolling up the newspaper.

"I am sure it will, very soon," Evan said, looking away. "Well, do let me know if you hear more." He had to think through his plan, and needed to get rid of his neighbor.

"I will, Mr. Daniels. Please do take care," the neighbor said turning around and walking down the front porch steps.

After the door closed, Evan turned around and grabbed his coat. He knew he had to take down the killer and blackmailer, who he believed were one in the same. He exited through the back door and went toward the cemetery, located down the hill from the house. He looked even further up the hill where the full moon's light was hitting the old Daniels Manor that sat the furthest up on the hill above the new Daniels estate.

He turned his attention back on the moonlit cemetery, scowering the landscape for a glimpse of movement. He walked around the cemetery hoping to make a discovery, but it was to no avail. Evan made his way home, deciding to visit the local cemeteries every night until he found the killer.

The next day, as he finished bathing, there came another knock at the door. Surprised, Evan quickly dried himself and hastily threw on his clothes. He ran downstairs and opened the door to find yet another package waiting for him. He looked around and didn't see anybody around this time. He picked up the box and went back inside, wondering what this box had in store for him. He opened the package and found another letter. The letter told him he had three days to give the blackmailer money, or he would run to the newspapers with evidence of Evan being a vampire. Feeling his rage growing ever more unstable he was determined to find this person and remove them from existence. He headed out just as night fell, trying to decide which cemetery to visit.

He came upon the oldest cemetery in town. As he crept around he saw nothing out of the ordinary, until he came to the back of the cemetery. He could hear voices. He saw a low glimmer of light coming from a crypt in the far back of the graveyard, and ran toward that area. He got there within seconds and crept slowly around the building.

He burst through the door and found a group of kids standing around a stone slab. The kids parted and Evan was horrified to find a young woman tied down to the stone. The kid up toward the woman's head had a small dagger, and appeared to be ready to plunge it into her chest. Evan ran toward him and knocked him down, grabbing the dagger out of his hand.

"What the hell are you doing," the women screamed from the stone slab.

"Trying to save your life," Evan said, still struggling with the kid under his knees.

"We're not trying to hurt her, she is becoming part of our group," the kid standing nearest to Evan said.

"What kind of group is this that has to kill someone for them to become a member," he asked, still kneeing the kid in the chest.

"We were only going to cut her hand and pour it into the cup and drink it, then she would be part of us," he said as he backed up a bit.

"Well, you're not going to be doing this sort of thing as long as I'm here," Evan said, standing up and wiping his coat off, "You guys need to get out of here now- there's a killer on the loose!"

"Not until you give me back my dagger," the boy on the floor yelled.

"You're not getting this back," Evan said, turning to leave.

"Don't make me hurt you buddy," the kid standing by the door said, as he grabbed Evan by the shoulder.

"Wrong move, *buddy*," Evan turned around, showed them his fangs and blacked- out eyes.

Without hesitation, the kids ran for the exit. Evan walked out of the crypt and watched them run out of the cemetery and towards town. Disappointed at not finding the mystery blackmailer, Evan left and went back home. He went into the front room and collapsed on the couch, still tired from the long night in the cemetery.

He woke up as the sun was setting again and decided tonight he would rest up for the next night. He heard a knock at the door and ran to answer it – curious to see if another package had arrived and hoping it would hold more clues as to who had sent it. He opened the door and looked down to find a package, then looked up just in time to see a guy walking out his front gate. Evan quickly dropped the package and darted down to the gate, catching the man before he had a chance to make his escape.

"Who are you and what do you want," Evan demanded, transforming his face.

"I'm not doing anything," the man proclaimed as he shook in Evan's hands, obviously terrified.

"Then who is putting you up to this," Evan asked, getting angrier.

"I don't know his name. He just pays me and drops off the packages to me without me even seeing him," he said, looking pale at this point.

"Fine, leave and never come back," Evan warned, pushing the guy out the gate.

Evan walked back up to the house and then turned around as he watched the guy run away. He couldn't figure out why or who would do this to him or who would even know what he was. He walked back up to the house and entered the already opened door. As he walked in a black shadow walked up behind him and hit him over the head, knocking him out cold.

Evan felt pain shoot down his head as his head banged off every step going toward the cellar. He knew he was in the cellar, smelling the musky, damp air of the crypt he had lived in for three years. He had slowly regained consciousness, until his head again dropped off the last step and ricocheted off the cement floor. He was in and out of consciousness, being dragged by a still unseen entity. He was just conscious enough to know that the person dragging him was taking him through the tunnels, up to the old manor.

He was right. When they entered the double doors leading into the cellar of the old manor, Evan woke up. Fully aware of his surroundings and feeling more stable, he was finally able to look around. All he could see was the pure blackness that was the manor's basement. He couldn't see his captor in the dark but could hear his footsteps walking farther away. Then out of the blackness came a loud bang and a metal scrapping sound. His captor returned and continued dragging him to where Evan had heard the noise. There in the wall was a gaping hole in which he was sure he was going to be locked up in. Evan was thrown into the hole and his captor followed him in. As Evan was feeling for something to prop himself up on, a light illuminated the space and he was finally able to see his captor.

"You! I figured you would have left this town," Evan said, shocked at what he saw.

"Nope I have just kept quiet until now," the creature said as he looked over Evan's face.

"Why are you doing this?"

"Because it was because of you I had to go into hiding," the creature began, "and also for ruining my good shirt that night."

“What does that have to do with anything,” Evan asked, looking puzzled.

“Nothing really, but it ticked me off,” the creature answered. “This town is not going to be big enough for two vampires so I figured I would get rid of my competition. Now enjoy a long and peaceful sleep….”

Evan didn’t know what to do, the creature he thought would be gone was now closing the steel door back into place and he couldn’t do anything about it. Then Evan remembered the dagger he had in his pocket from earlier. He grabbed ahold of the dagger and ran straight at the creature, plunging the dagger into the creature’s eye. He pulled the dagger out and dragged the creature into the room, pulling the creature’s head back and quickly working to sever his head off. When Evan was finished, the creature’s body turned to ash. As Evan turned, the door was still closing and latched before he could get to it. Evan was trapped. He had no way of knowing how long he would have to wait before someone would find the hidden hatch.

Chapter Four

Present Day

Phineas Daniels loved the Canadian countryside. He had lived there for several years on his family's land. He had contemplated moving back to the states where his brother lived, but had decided against it. The beauty and comfort of his home were much too much to leave behind, even if it was for something like family.

This particular morning had been just as any other morning. Phineas watched out his study window as the fog was rolling down the hills away from his house. He drank his cup of coffee, preparing to take his dogs running in the woods that surrounded his home.

He walked into the woods and watched as his dogs went running around in different directions. As they got further into the woods, the darker it became – almost becoming difficult to see where the dogs had gone on ahead of him. Phineas was sipping his coffee and watching through the woods when he heard a loud noise come from his left. He looked toward the left and heard the noise again, but this time it came from the right. It was as if something was circling him, but what it was he couldn't be sure.

"Hello," he said, almost as a question, trying to make contact with whoever, or whatever, was there in the woods with him. No answer came back as he became more and more nervous, looking around cautiously.

Then one of Phineas' dogs jumped out from behind a tree and scared him. After letting out a quick yell, he quickly kneeled down and ruffled the dog's fur, laughing at his own paranoia. He stood back up, and was hit on the right side by a creature. He looked up at it as it came at him again. It had the physical characteristics of a wolf, but looked like a human. Half dazed from the surprise of the attack, he had trouble believing what he was seeing. He tried to push the beast off him but it was much stronger than he realized. His dogs started to run toward the creature and attacked the beast. The dogs were able to subdue the creature allowing Phineas to get back on his feet. He grabbed a large branch off one of the trees and started beating the creature with it. The creature finally collapsed, but not before sending the last remaining dog to its death by throwing it against a tree. Phineas watched as the beast died, then, in a state of shock, walked back to the edge of the woods. As Phineas left the scene of the attack, the beast transformed into a man, lying dead on the ground.

When he reached the edge of the woods, he noticed the blood pouring out of his chest where the beast had scratched him. He walked back to his house, pulled out some towels and went into the bathroom to wash off the blood. He had cleaned his wounds the best he could and wrapped his upper body with medical gauze wraps. When he finished, he looked at himself in the mirror, exhausted and not knowing what to do with the information going through his mind at the moment. Starring back at him was a man in his mid-thirties, with black medium-length hair, grayish-blue eyes and a muscular face. He rubbed his forehead where the creature had hit him. He didn't know what had attacked him, but he couldn't help but feel like it had all been a dream…just a horrible nightmare. The unanswered questions were just too much for him, so he went into his bedroom and gently fell into his bed…hoping some sleep would help bring sense to it all.

Two weeks later, he found himself no closer to finding any answers. Just when he was about to chalk it up to nothing more than a wolf attack, he found himself stricken with a fever and stomach pains. He didn't know what it was that was causing the new symptoms, but he couldn't shake the feeling that it was related to the attack, even though much time had passed. He called his doctor and the doctor replied that is was most likely a virus and presumably not related to the wolf attack. He listened to the doctor, drank lots of fluids and rested, but there was no relief. In fact, the fever and pain continued to worsen – the pain itself nearly unbearable. As bad as things were, Phineas had no clue what he was in for.

As the full moon rose in the sky, nearly a month after the attack, Phineas' pain became excruciating. He felt the muscles in his body contract, then feel as if they were about to rip open. His legs elongated, making a sound like strained rubber bands. His toes reset themselves, becoming paw-like, as the tips ripped open to reveal long, deadly claws. His back went rigid as his spine stretched and curved, and his shoulder muscles bulged out making his back appear very large. His shoulders cracked and widened, as his arms moved down into a slightly lower positions. His fingers become longer, flesh tearing off to reveal another set of claws. His jaw unhinged, stretching to accommodate the sharp canine-like teeth that now occupied his mouth. His face twisted and contorted in pain, his eyes shot open revealing eyes that were green and glaring. His ears moved up and lengthened as a thick coat of fur quickly flowed out of his skin, now covering his entire body.

The transformation was complete. Phineas no longer had control over his body; he had become the very beast that had attacked him, and the beast within took control. He broke through the front window and took off down the hill towards the town below.

The next morning Phineas awoke in the middle of his study, lying in a pool of blood. He felt unusually groggy, vaguely remembering what had happened the night before. He only remembered the painful transformation, which made him shudder. He ran to the bathroom and jumped in the shower, washing away the blood as if that would make the whole experience wash away as well. He dried off and walked into the study, looking at the broken window and wondering what other atrocities he had committed.

Once he finished cleaning up the blood in his study, he headed to the kitchen to call about repairing the window. As he entered the kitchen, he clicked on the television. Just as he began to dial a number, he heard a news report about the terror that had struck the town overnight. With a sinking feeling, he dropped the phone and his eyes widened with shock as the news story unfolded before him.

The night before there were three killings that took place in the town just down the road from his house. It was said the bodies were ripped apart and that the culprit was most likely a large animal of some kind. He turned off the television and went back to the phone. Anxiously, he dialed a number and a voicemail message answered. He waited for the prompt and left a message.

"Melanie, please contact me when you get back from vacation. I need your help and I don't know where to turn…I will be going to my brother's house in the states if you could just come there. I believe you know where it is…please…hurry," he said as he hung up the phone.

Phineas ran upstairs and started packing up some of his belongings, then ran out the door of his house. He got in his car and sped off to the airport hoping to get a quick flight to the states.

Hayden Daniels had lived in the Daniels' estate for several years. The house and surrounding estate was going to be torn down if a Daniels didn't occupy it. Hayden, despising the thought of losing such an important part of his family's history, decided to move in. He lived there with his three kids, wife and his sister. They all thoroughly loved their home. Hayden found himself to have a connection to the house, more so than just the fact that his ancestors had built it and lived there for generations. He had been drawn to it, and knew without a doubt that this is where he would spend the rest of his life.

On that dark, rainy day, Hayden was sitting in the den, watching as the rain poured from the clouds. He noticed a cab pulling up at the front gate, and a man in a long winter jacket stepping out, hunched over as he grabbed his luggage from the cab. Hayden continued to watch as the man walked up the long sidewalk that led to the house.

The man walking up toward the front door looked as if he was down on his luck. His long winter coat flapped in the wind and his hair was messy and chaotic looking. He was hunched over as if he had a hangover he was trying to shake from the night before. As he got to the door he sat the luggage down and leaned up against the door frame and started to knock when the door opened.

Hayden opened the door and was disturbed by the appearance of the man on the other side of the door. “May I help you sir,” he asked, hoping he could easily get rid of this odd character.

“You don’t even recognize your own brother,” Phineas said, as he lifted his head up from the doorframe. “Nice house you have here by the way.”

“Phineas? Is that you,” Hayden looked at his brother in disbelief.

“Yeah, it’s me,” he paused looking for the words to say, “I was wondering if I could move in with you, just until I get my life back on track.”

"Well, I don't have a bedroom for you to sleep in, but you could stay in the basement," he said as he looked behind him, then back toward Phineas. He continued to look over his brother, wondering how he could have possibly ended up in this condition. He loved his brother, and even if he didn't have the answers yet, he couldn't leave his brother to pick up the pieces of his life on his own.

"The basement will work just fine," Phineas said as he picked up his bags and headed through the door past Hayden.

"The basement is that door on the left," Hayden said pointing, while also closing the front door.

"One more question," Phineas stopped, hunched over in the hall looking back at his brother, "is there any wooded areas around these parts?"

"Well, there's Daniels Moore up over Infirmary Hill, past the Daniels Manor," Hayden said as he rubbed his head, thinking.

“Ok, that’s all I needed and also…thanks,” Phineas said as he opened the basement door and proceeded down the stairs.

Chapter Five

Phineas Daniels had been living in his brother's basement for about a month. As time went on, he began to make his surroundings more of a home, cleaning and organizing the basement. He decided he would work on organizing the shelf that was directly across from his bed so he could put some books on it. As he was cleaning it off, he noticed the shelf moved back slightly as he pushed on it. He became curious and pushed a little harder, revealing an opening in the wall. He spotted a lantern on the floor by his bed and picked it up. He shook the lantern and listened for the sloshing of the lamp oil. When he heard there was still oil in the lantern, he pulled out a lighter and lit it. He turned around and went into the space, leaving the doorway open. Thinking it was more of a storage area, he was shocked to find that it was actually a tunnel. He kept moving forward, moving his free hand along the cobwebbed covered walls.

The tunnel kept going for what seemed like a mile, ending at an iron door. He pushed on it and it creaked open. The light from the lantern crawled across the floor and opposite wall. He entered farther into the room and began to look around. It was obvious the room had been closed up for some time. Finally he reached the opposite wall and decided to turn back around and take the view of the whole room in. As he did this he leaned against the wall, popping it open and sliding it out of the way. Phineas fell straight back and his lantern went behind him, rolling on the floor. When he looked up he saw the eerie glow of a face in the back corner. Phineas went to run but was grabbed by the shoulder.

"Wait, don't leave," the person said, holding on tightly.

"Who, who are you," Phineas asked, picking up the lantern and holding it up to the person's face.

"My name is Evan Daniels," he began, "and what is your name, sir?"

"Mine is Phineas Daniels," Phineas answered back, looking perplexed.

"I need an animal to feed on," Evan said, holding onto the wall.

"An animal," Phineas asked, confused by such an odd request. He stood and began making his way back out to the main room.

"How long have I been locked up in there," Evan asked as he exited the room as well.

"Not sure when you were locked up, but the year is 2012," Phineas answered back.

"It's been just a little over a hundred years then," Evan said as he sat on a cement slab that was in the middle of the basement.

Phineas began processing all that he had heard and seen in the past few minutes. It soon started to become clear to him how this man could still be alive and why he would be asking for an animal to eat. "I am taking it you must be a vampire," Phineas stated, jumping after a rat for Evan.

"That I am," Evan began, "and you don't seem overly surprised or shocked by this."

"Believe me, you're not the only one that knows about weird stuff," Phineas said as he handed over the dead rat to Evan.

"Thank you," Evan said, taking it and then biting into the small rodent, letting the blood flow over his tongue and down his throat.

"Well, we'll have to introduce you to my brother…but how." Phineas asked walking back and forth in front of Evan.

"You're brother," Evan inquired.

"Yes, my brother, Hayden. He owns the Daniels' estate now. I've been living with him for about a month now," Phineas explained.

"Daniels," Evan restated. "I must be your ancestor then? Feels odd to say that…"

"I can imagine. So, my brother…how should we introduce you to him," Phineas asked again.

"Perhaps we could say I'm a friend of yours," Evan suggested.

"That might work…or better yet, why not say you're a relative of ours? We could say that we met on one of those family tree websites and I invited you here," Phineas said, stopping and looking at Evan.

"Website," Evan asked.

"Yeah, well, a lot has changed in one hundred years…I'll get you caught up on that stuff later. For now, we need to find your some more current clothes before you meet my brother."

"And I can live up here for the time being," Evan said, looking around.

"That might work," Phineas said, "I'll go get some of my clothes and bring them back for you to wear."

"I shall wait here," Evan said, getting up and walking around.

Evan began looking around the basement and then went upstairs to investigate. He noticed as he got up the stairs that someone had been doing some renovating. He walked into the den and was astonished at how clean it was. Even back in his time, the Manor was not in the best of shape. He made his way into the kitchen and opened up the cabinets. They were stocked with food. As he came upon the entrance way, Phineas came running up behind Evan holding some clothes.

"Wow, it's just me," Phineas said putting up his hand.

“Are you unaware that sneaking up on a vampire is a bad idea,” Evan asked, putting his fangs away.

“Sorry, but here are some clothes,” Phineas handed over the clothes to Evan, “I have to get back down to the house and act surprised when you show up. Do you remember the story?”

“Yes, I am a relative that you met on a family tree web?” Evan asked Phineas, thinking about it.

“Website. Family tree website,” Phineas reminded him, turning and going back down the basement stairs. “Give me about thirty minutes and start heading down the hill.”

“Ok, I will,” Evan said as he began unbuttoning his shirt.

Chapter Six

After Evan had got dressed, he sat behind the desk in the den waiting for the time to leave. He looked over the books in the book cases and discovered most of them were original to the house. He was very surprised that the books had survived that long without being cared for. After standing up to analyze the books, Evan decided it had been long enough and headed for the front door.

The fall air was starting to settle in and Evan could tell the fall festival had begun from the lights coming from the middle of the town, though it looked much brighter than he ever remembered it. He wondered what had changed since he had last been out of the house. He heard new noises, and experienced new smells. He noticed people traveling by without horse-drawn carriages, instead passing by in large metal contraptions. He had a lot to learn about this new world around him. Until he did, he would have to keep his wits about him and remain calm, not to bring attention to himself by being shocked or surprised by the more modern marvels.

Evan descended the long, overgrown stairs down to the Daniels' Estate. The wind began to pick up, blowing leaves around as he stepped up onto the porch. He pulled the coat closer to him, recalling the night so many years ago that started just like this. He reached out his hand to knock on the door.

Hayden Daniels was enjoying his dinner with his family when he heard a faint knock on the door. As he got up from his chair, he noticed his brother sitting at the opposite end of the table with his head up in the air as if he was trying to sniff an invisible smell. Hayden turned back toward the door, walked up to it and peered out. On the other side of the door was a well dressed man who appeared to be unkempt. He pulled the door open and was shocked as his brother came running up beside him.

"Hello, how may I help you sir," greeted Hayden as the door creaked further open.

"Yes, I am Evan Daniels and I am here to see Phineas Daniels," Evan said quite easily.

"Oh, Hayden I forgot to tell you that before I came here I was doing research on our family and I met a distant cousin of ours," Phineas began as he pushed Hayden out of the way, "Evan here was hoping to get some more information on our family. I invited him here so we could study our family tree."

"Let's go into the den and talk more in private shall we," Hayden said leading the way.

"Let's do that," Phineas said turning and giving Evan a wink.

As they all went into the den, Evan noticed little had changed since he was forced to leave the house that night by the creature who cursed him. The chairs were located in the same place and he took the chair his mother had been in the night he killed her.

"So where do you come from Evan? I thought we were the only Daniels left in America," Hayden said as he took his seat.

"Well that's what I thought about myself as well until I met Phineas here and he told me about his brother who lived in America. But I am just a distant cousin of the family that lived here."

"We too are distant cousins," said Hayden looking toward Phineas.

"So I see," Evan said as he looked over at Phineas.

"We have been talking for like the last six months and I told him I was coming to visit you, and he should come as well so we can research family history together," Phineas explained, jumping in on the conversation.

"Well, that is a mighty fine idea," Hayden began, "Do you have a place to stay Evan?"

"Actually, that was something else we were talking about," Phineas spoke up.

"Yes, I was wondering if perhaps I could stay up in the old Manor for the time being," Evan asked as he stood to look at the picture of his mother and father that hung over the fireplace, "I figured there might be some history up there."

"That is fine with me," Hayden began as he stood up as well, "I have been trying to fix the place up a little bit at a time, so you will find some food up in the pantries if you are hungry. But sadly there is no electric up there yet so you will have to use candles and lanterns for the time being."

"That shall be fine," Evan said turning around to face Hayden, "That should make the family search that much more fun. Think about it researching our relatives only using the light they would have had."

"I think I might stay with Evan up in the Manor, if that is ok," Phineas said, looking over toward Hayden.

"Yeah, I hope you guys find what you are looking for," Hayden said as he went toward the window, "Not to alarm you, but I have heard rumors that there are ghost up in the old Manor as well."

"Oh I am not afraid of ghosts," Evan said, glancing at Phineas, "The ghosts should be afraid of me."

"I do know some of our family history and one thing that has been said was that way back in the early 19th century, our family built that manor. Then after the Civil War, they built this house and moved most of their belongings down here and closed up that house. Nobody knows why they did this but rumor has it they did it because they were haunted by ghosts and didn't want to live up there anymore," Hayden said as he continued to look out the window.

"Well, before the Daniels moved to this area, there was an Infirmary placed upon that hill, hence the name Infirmary Hill. It was around the 1830's that our family purchased the land and tore down the Infirmary to build the Manor. There have been rumors that between here and the Manor there is an unmarked graveyard holding the bodies of the Infirmary patients," Evan said, looking more seriously at Hayden.

"Those are some very interesting facts," Hayden began as he turned away from the window, "Well, like I said, I hope you guys find some more information on our family."

"Oh I am sure we will," Phineas said, pulling on Evan's arm.

"Well I suppose I shall take my leave up to the Manor," Evan said as he turned to follow Phineas.

“If you need anything at all just come down and get me. I am always willing to help,” Hayden said as he saw Evan and Phineas out the front door.

“That went well,” Evan said to Phineas as they walked off the porch.

“Yeah I think so,” Phineas started, “I am going to go get my belongings in the basement and I will meet you up there in a few minutes.”

“Ok, then you can educate me on what has become of this world,” Evan said, approaching the steps.

As Evan walked up the steps toward the Manor he was thinking over his conversation with Hayden. He was so impressed with the knowledge he had about their family. He was thinking about this when he looked up just in time to see a black figure move quickly by the front entrance door. Thinking it was just Phineas coming from the basement tunnel, he thought nothing of it. He grabbed ahold of the door knob and opened the door slowly.

"Phineas, is that you," Evan asked, getting no answer.

After getting no answer, he figured that Phineas must have forgotten something down in the basement. He walked into the entrance hallway and found a candelabra sitting on a stand with matches lying beside it. Evan lit the candles and began walking up the stairs just to see how the house was laid out. When he got to the top of the steps, the front door opened and Phineas walked in. Evan turned around on the steps and walked down them, surprised to see Phineas coming through the front door.

"Why are you coming through the front door," Evan asked, still surprised.

"What do you mean," Phineas asked as he put down his belongings.

"I mean, weren't you just here," Evan asked, pointing down the stairs.

"No, I just left the house down there," Phineas said, pointing over his shoulder.

"I swear I saw a shadow move in this house when I got up to the door," Evan said, shaking his head.

"Maybe it's just because you're still thirsting for more blood," Phineas said, picking up his bags again and heading into the den.

"Maybe that's it," Evan said again, shaking his head, still unsure about what he had seen.

"I need your help, Evan," Phineas asked, coming back into the entrance way.

"What is it," Evan asked. He set the candles back on the stand in the hallway and turned back towards Phineas.

"Well I was hoping you could help me figure that part out," Phineas said while watching the fire from the candles dance.

"Ok, how may I be of assistance?"

"Well, I was attacked by a creature about a month ago, and on the full moon of last month, I became the creature that attacked me," Phineas said, looking nervously from the floor to Evan while biting his fingernails.

"Are you telling me you turn into a werewolf," Evan said, looking deeply interested.

"So you know what I am talking about then," said Phineas, perking up.

"Well, I have only heard a little about werewolves, and most of that is only from legends. Nothing from first-hand accounts," Evan said, rubbing his chin.

"Well I can assure you it's no longer legend, it's real."

"I believe you, I could tell when we met early there was something different about you."

"So do you think you can help me with this," asked Phineas, looking back into the flames.

"Well I can try to do some research on werewolves, but I do not know how helpful I can be. I'll do my best. Do you know anyone else with knowledge of these sorts of things? Anyone at all?"

"Well…I have a friend who is really into this sort of stuff. I called her last month and asked her for help, but so far she has yet to return my calls."

"Well that's because it took me a while to get over to the States," said Melanie, as she walked through the opened door. Both Phineas and Evan looked up at her, startled. She was tall and slender, with red hair, and fair skin. She wore dark make-up – purple, gray and black – and a black lace shirt with a long black skirt and knee-high black boots. It was obvious from looking at her that she would have an interest in dark matters, though even with her gothic style, she had an heir of elegance about her.

"Melanie, you're here!" Phineas exclaimed, running to hug his friend.

"Your brother told me that you were up here visiting your cousin, so I figured I would come up here and see you. You sounded urgent on the phone."

"Yeah, that's actually why I'm here talking to my cousin. A problem has arisen," Phineas said, then smacking his hand to his forehead, he continued, "Oh, geez, where are my manners? Melanie this is Evan, Evan this is Melanie," Phineas said, gesturing to each of them.

"Hi, nice to meet you," Evan said reaching out his hand.

"Same here," Melanie reached out her hand. "Wait – there is something different about you. You too, Phineas. The both of you have something odd happening with your energy. What's going on here?" she asked, looking between the two of them.

"Shall we convene in the dinning room? I will see if I can find anything for us to drink, then we can talk," Evan said as he pointed into the next room.

"Thanks, but I'm good. Got a bottle of water in my bag," Melanie said, as she reached into her large tote and pulled out the bottle.

"Phineas, what about you? Do you…want anything to drink?"

"No, I am ok for now," Phineas said, anxiously looking down toward the ground.

"Well, shall we begin then? We have several things to talk about," Evan said as he led the way.

The group talked through everything. Vampires, werewolves – all of it. It was nearly morning when they had finished telling Melanie about each of their lives, and what amounted to basically being the end of their lives and beginning of a new life. She sat there, still, unable to believe that someone so near and dear to her was deep in the middle of the very things that she found so fascinating. She was both unnerved and thrilled.

"So…you're a vampire – and you are a werewolf," she said, pointing to each of them.

"Yes, that is about the gist of it," Evan said as he got up from the table.

"But now that you guys know about me being a werewolf, there's something I have to ask you," Phineas said, looking up at the two of them.

"What would that be," Evan said crossing his arms.

"Tonight is the full moon and I want you guys to lock me up so I can't hurt anybody."

"I know the perfect place," said Evan.

"Ok while you guys go take care of that, I will go and find out all I can about werewolves from my contacts," Melanie said, as she joined Evan and Phineas standing.

"We need to all meet back in the basement of the Daniels Estate," Evan said as he moved toward one of the windows in the dining room. "But before we do that I need some help from both of you as well."

"Ok, what do you need help with," Melanie asked, looking over at Evan.

"Well, since I just 'woke' up I need new clothes," Evan said as he walked back to the table. “I don’t have money, obviously, but there is a large safe in this house that I was told held many jewels of the Daniels family. If there was a way to sell them, then I could get money for items I need.”

“Do you mean like a pawn shop,” Phineas said, crossing his arms, interested to hear of a family treasure.

“Perhaps,” Evan answered, uncertainly.

“Ok, let’s go get some of these old heirlooms and when I am out I will pawn them and get you some clothes,” Melanie said, moving around to the entry way. “You look like you’re about the same size as Phineas, so I should be able to find you some clothes pretty easily.”

“Thanks for this,” Evan said, as he turned and ran up the stairs to fetch the old jewels from the safe.

As Evan was doing this, Phineas and Melanie were waiting in the entry way for his return. Phineas slowly leaned in for a kiss from Melanie, she leaned into him and they embraced.

They hadn't noticed Evan return until he cleared his throat.

"I didn't realize you two were, um, together," Evan said, standing on the stairs.

"Yeah, we have been going out for a few years now," Melanie replied.

"Oh, well, that's great to hear. Uh, anyway, here are some jewels. I hope they will be enough," Evan said, handing over a handful of very old and rare jewels.

"Ooh, these should fetch a pretty penny," Phineas said, looking closely at the jewels, in awe of their size and beauty.

"Is there any certain types of clothes you would like," Melanie asked, looking from the jewels back to Evan.

"Hmm, white dress shirts, black slacks, a dress coat and a long black winter coat if you don't mind. And, I suppose, other clothing that is considered modern for this time," Evan said, looking at Melanie and Phineas.

"Ok, I will take care of the jewels, get the clothes and get back to meet you guys in the basement then," Melanie said, walking through the front door.

"Thanks," Evan said as he shut the door behind them.

They all separated and started working on their individual steps of their plan. As the day grew into night, the three of them got back together to share what they discovered. As Evan entered the basement through the tunnel, the memories came flooding back to him – locking himself into the crypt so that he could overcome his bloodlust.

"Well, I did as much research as I could about werewolves, but most of it we've already heard – full moon, transformation caused by attack – just the usual stuff," said Melanie as she reached into her pocket and pulled out a silver ring. "But, there was a person who gave me this. He said it was a tribal ring, a few centuries old, that would make the person who was turning into the werewolf able to control when he turned except, on the full moon, but that person would be able to have more control over the beast once he turned."

"I'll take that," said Phineas as he grabbed the silver ring. He turned it over, looking at it carefully. It was an obvious antique, sterling silver, with a wolf's head engraved into it.

"I'm sure it's a lovely ring, but in case it doesn't work, you need to get into here," Evan said, as he opened up the door to the family crypt.

"This should be fun," Phineas said, walking through the door.

"We will see you in the morning," Evan said as he shut the heavy metal door.

"Oh, Evan…I have your clothes upstairs if you would like to go try them on," Melanie said pointing up the stairs.

"Ok, I will do that," Evan said as he went sprinting up the stairs.

Evan was gone not more than five minutes when he came down the basement stairs dressed in his new duds. Melanie was checking out the fit of the clothes as he walked closer to her.

"I think they fit perfectly," Melanie said as she looked him up and down.

"Yes, they are quite comfortable," Evan said, pulling on his new sport coat.

"By the way, here's your money that was left over," Melanie said, handing over a thick stack of cash and a check to Evan.

"Wow, how much is there," Evan asked looking surprised.

"Well, after buying the clothes, I would say about five hundred thousand. There's about $2,000 in cash there, then the check shows the rest. We'll have to set up a bank account for you to hold the money. Asking to cash a check for that much money gets you a funny look, so that's not really an option," Melanie answered.

"That's just amazing, and there's even more jewels up there in that old safe," Evan said, still looking in shock at the stack of cash.

"I would say you are probably set for a good while then," Melanie said, thinking of the amount of money still locked up in that safe.

"I guess," Evan said, sitting down on the floor opposite Phineas' bed.

Evan and Melanie sat in the basement as the night dragged on. They heard the painful transformation and the growls coming from within the crypt. They continued to share their life stories until Melanie thought it would be a good idea to go and get something to eat. Even though Evan couldn't eat regular food, he decided to go with her knowing Phineas was locked up and safe.

As Melanie and Evan returned to the estate, the sun was just beginning to rise behind the heavy fog. They entered into the basement and noticed the tunnel door was wide open. A streak of blood ran from the tunnel to the family crypt.

The door was open to the crypt as well and lying there, half naked, was Phineas. Evan and Melanie knew this couldn't be a good sign.

Chapter Seven

The fall air was crisp as the town's fall festival was coming to an end. As the booths closed up shop and prepared to move on to other festivals, the gypsies had one place on their mind – Daniels' Moore.

"So are we going to go to Daniels' Moore," a woman asked, sitting in the front of a carriage.

"Yes, as we have always done and our ancestors have done before us," a guy said, driving the carriage up the road toward Infirmary Hill.

As the caravan of wagons made their way up the road, the full moon came out from behind the clouds and lit up the path of the road. The caravan made their way to the cemetery, passing the oldest part of it. As the gypsies came closer to their destination, singing broke out among the caravan. It was truly going to be a celebration…of sorts.

The wagons came to a stop, encircling a cleared area of ground. They set their wagons up and had them facing each other. Some of the guys went and collected fire wood and placed it in the circle between the wagons. They doused the wood with alcohol and lit the fire. Soon music started flowing freely.

As the night progressed, the music changed tones several times. As the fire was slowly dying down and the singing all but stopped, a gypsy woman turned and began to ask a question to one of the men playing music.

"What is the legend about these woods again," she asked, as she looked around to the other gypsies.

"Well, the story begins around a hundred years ago, when a creature attacked our ancestors in these woods," he said as people gathered around to hear the tale. Continuing to lightly strum his guitar, he continued, "As it is said in myths, a creature, after attacking the fall festival, followed our ancestors to these woods, where it attacked them as well. A lucky few managed to survive as the creature moved up to the Daniels' Estate."

"They killed the creature, right," asked the young gypsy woman.

"No. They say, after it killed the Daniels family, it came back to the woods and still roams 'til this very day."

The wind picked up and blew the remainder of the fire out. Everyone jumped and then started to laugh, amused by their jitteriness. Then, as everything began to quiet down once again, they heard a noise in the woods behind the wagons. They listened intently to where the noise came from; a distant howling spooked all of them. They ran to their wagons and refused to look out their windows.

While the groups stayed in their wagons, a scream ripped through the fall air. The creature was now in the camp, slowly creeping around the wagons. Suddenly, it started ripping through each one of the wagons. The gypsies in the surrounding wagons jumped into action, trying to escape. The creature started to claw and rip through people as they tried to run by it unnoticed. As a few of the wagons were racing back down the trail, the lead wagon was suddenly toppled over from the force of the creature hitting into it.

As the creature tore into the wagon and pulled out each person one by one, the other carriages sped off around the creature. The creature looked up and saw the other wagons getting away. Frustrated, he stood up and howled toward the sky. Finished with his hunt, he started back toward the Daniels Manor on the hill. The moon shone brightly on the hill, illuminating the hairy beast as he turned and glanced back down the hill at the carnage that lay below.

Chapter Eight

After Evan and Melanie got Phineas covered up and propped up on his bed, the questions started to fly.

"How could this have happened," Melanie broke the silence, pacing the floor.

"I don't know. That crypt held me, and being a vampire, well…I thought I'd be stronger than a werewolf would be," Evan said, looking up to Melanie.

"I doubt that Evan. I can take you anytime, anywhere," Phineas said as he tried to straighten himself up on the bed.

"You do know what werewolves were used for, don't you Phineas," Melanie asked. Phineas shrugged his shoulders. "They were once the right-hand-men of the vampires - being they were able to walk around during the day. So, I am pretty sure Evan can take you, especially since he is like a hundred years old which makes him stronger. But, enough of this bickering about who's bigger, stronger…we need to figure out how Phineas got out, and what or who he killed."

"Well I examined the lock and it appears to be cut from the outside, so it almost seems like someone let him out," Evan said looking toward the crypt.

"There's only one place he could have went through – that tunnel – and that's up to your house," Melanie said, looking through the dark tunnel.

"Well it doesn't end there," Evan paused, "it also splits off and leads out the hill and into Daniels Moore."

"So whatever happened probably happened in the Moore," Melanie paused to think, "We should probably get down there."

"Ok, we should go and let him rest," Evan said, as he stood up and looked back around at Phineas.

"That sounds good to me," Phineas said as he fell over onto the bed.

Evan and Melanie made their way through the dark tunnel toward the manor. As they came closer to the manor, Evan made a sudden left turn and entered through another door that led to the Moore. Melanie followed close behind, looking at the trail of blood that lined the tunnel's floor.

They came to the door that opened up into the side of the hill. It was a steep drop, but before they even made it down they could see the damage that had been done. Bodies were scattered everywhere. Wagons were overturned and blood was all over the ground. Melanie looked at Evan and then back to the blood.

"Does this bother you, all this blood," she said stepping in front of him.

"No. I learned a long time ago how to control my urges to feed off of human blood," he said, looking from the ground up to her.

"Well I am glad to hear that," she said with a nervous chuckle.

"We should get back to looking around," Evan said as he started scanning the ground.

The ground was covered in blood and internal organs from the people who had been camping there the night before. As Evan scanned the ground, he saw the wolf ring that Melanie gave to Phineas the night before. He slowly picked up the ring and twirled it around in his fingers. With his heightened sense of smell, he sniffed the ring.

"The ring you gave Phineas last night," Evan said, handing it to Melanie.

“So that proves that Phineas did all of this,” she said looking at the ring in her hand.

“Not exactly, it doesn’t have Phineas’ scent on it,” Evan said as he looked at Melanie, “it smells familiar, but not Phineas.”

“Then someone is trying to set Phineas up, but who,” she wondered, as she looked at Evan.

“I don’t know, but we need to find out soon, before the trail of bodies leads back to us,” Evan said. Pausing, he turned his head toward the hill, “Quick, jump on my back.”

“Why?”

“Just do it,” he said, turning his back toward her.

She jumped on his back and Evan went flying back up the hill. They reached the tunnel door. Evan quickly closed the door and put his ear up against it. Melanie was confused at first, until she heard the sirens from the police cars approaching the Moore.

"It seems our time is running out," Melanie whispered up to Evan.

"It appears we need to start working on this….now," Evan said, as he turned and walked pass Melanie.

"And how are we suppose to do that," Melanie yelled after him.

"Well, for one, I am going down there to talk with the police," he said, looking over his shoulders toward Melanie.

"No! You can't do that! It will draw suspicion to the Daniels," she said running after him.

"No it won't. I am just a concerned citizen wondering what's going on," he said as he ascended his basement stairs.

"Please don't go down there. It is going to ruin our investigation," she said, stopping at the Manor's front door.

"The best way to get information is to help the police out," he said, pulling his winter coat on as he descended the front porch stairs.

Melanie just stood there and rolled her eyes at him. He walked around the house and had a great view of the entire scene. As he began to walk down the hill, he noticed one of the cops looking up at him. He looked back and waved, getting a nod in return. As he made his way down the hill, the police were waiting at the bottom for his arrival as if they were going to question him.

"Hello, gentlemen," Evan said, nodding his head toward the police.

As Evan got closer to the scene, the lead investigator turned and started to walk toward him.

"May I help you sir," he said, looking at Evan with a crude look on his face.

"Oh, I am just wondering what happened down here. I live in that house on the hill up there and heard the sirens," Evan said pointing toward the house on the hill above.

"Did you see what happened here last night," the investigator asked, coming closer to Evan.

"No, I was actually at my cousin's house, down the hill, with a friend last night so I wasn't home most of the night."

"I am taking it you're a Daniels then," he said, with a slight mocking tone to his voice.

"Yes, I moved here just a few days ago," Evan said, looking around at all the cops as they searched the grounds.

"What's your name, sir," the investigator asked as he opened up his notebook to begin writing.

"It's Evan Daniels, just moved here from across the states," Evan said extending his hand to shake.

"I hope you don't mind if I check out your story, do you," the investigator asked closing his notebook.

"I don't mind, I have others who will corroborate my whereabouts," Evan said, dropping his hand.

"Sir, you should see this," a police officer said, holding something small and covered in blood.

"What is it," he said as he stepped closer to the police officer.

"It's a driver's license for a Phineas Daniels," he said, extending his hand toward the investigator.

"Is this the so-called cousin you were visiting with last night," the investigator asked turning toward Evan.

"Well yes, that's the one I was visiting with and I was there all night, so he couldn't have been out here," Evan said, hoping to cover Phineas's tracks.

"Well I will see about that, Mr. Daniels," he said looking back at the police officer.

"I'm afraid I must be off…very busy day ahead of me," Evan said as he began walking away.

"If I were you, Mr. Daniels, I wouldn't go too far. I am sure I will be in contact with you again."

"Since I live here now, I am sure I will not be going anywhere anytime soon," Evan said, continuing to look up the hill.

As Evan began toward the front of his house, he began to think of ways to get Phineas out of this mess. He looked up to see Melanie standing on the front porch, waiting on him.

"Did you find anything out," she asked, while looking down at her hand as if she had something in her nails.

"No, except they found Phineas's drivers license down there in the blood," Evan said, looking up at her through squinted eyes.

"Well we need to figure out a way to either hide Phineas or clear his name," Melanie said, wringing her hands nervously.

They sat down on the front porch steps and began to brainstorm ideas but nothing, it seemed, would work. As they were thinking, they saw the police cars pull up in front of the Daniels Estate and they knew this was not a good sign. Evan pulled on Melanie's hand, coming down from the porch and descending the hill toward the house below.

When they arrived, the police were carrying out Phineas trying to control him. He was shouting and trying to jerk away from the police officers, but to no avail. Evan saw the scared look in Phineas' eyes, and went running into the house to find the same investigator he had ran into earlier.

"What the hell do you think you're doing with my cousin," Evan flew into the man who had his cousin in cuffs.

"Well, you're lucky I am not arresting you for lying to an investigator," he said looking back at Hayden who was sitting in the den as well. "Your other cousin paints a different picture of what happened last night. He says the three of you went to the basement, and he woke up this morning to find only you two coming back into the house. So where was your cousin during that time?"

A long pause awaited the investigator's answer. Evan was trying to control his anger, but he was almost to the point of turning this man into his next meal.

"That's what I thought…no answer," he said putting his notepad away, "And by the way, don't go too far. I am sure as this case plays out that you're involved somehow."

Evan just rolled his eyes and began to calm down. Melanie saw how tense Evan was getting. She grabbed his shoulder and squeezed, hoping to relieve some of that tension. As the investigator left, Evan turned his anger toward Hayden, who was just sitting there, shocked.

"Why couldn't you have lied," Evan ripped into him.

“They told me what they found and I couldn’t believe it. They asked me where my brother was last night and I had to tell them the truth,” Hayden said in a rushed pace.

“Well you said you woke up to us coming in this morning, but you were awake when we went out, so why didn’t you tell them that,” Evan said looking back at Melanie.

“I didn’t think of it. Yes I admit that I was up when you left, but what does that have to do with anything,” he asked, looking at the two of them.

“I don’t know, but it sure seems like your hiding something and we’re going to find it out,” Evan said looking back at Hayden with hate in his eyes.

Evan and Melanie turned back around and walked out the door. As they were heading back up to Evan’s place, Evan couldn’t help but think about what Hayden was hiding. He knew he was hiding something from his body language and lack of eye contact.

"So what are we going to do now," Melanie asked looking up at Evan.

"Well we need to investigate this more and look into Hayden more-something doesn't add up about him," Evan said as he turned around and looked back down the hill.

"Well my little sister is a good investigator, I could always call her in."

"Ok, and we can use the money you got from the jewels to help pay the bail," Evan said pulling out the money from the inside pocket of his long black winter coat.

"I won't be long," Melanie said walking out on the hill overlooking the cemetery below.

As Melanie looked out over the cemetery she noticed the dark blue clouds laying on the horizon as the chilly fall air began to blow around her. When she got off the phone with her sister she just stood there, admiring the scenery and trying to clear her mind from the past two days' events. As she was slowly forgetting, she turned to see Evan coming toward her, the wind making his winter jacket flap around him.

"So, is your sister coming to help us out?"

"Yeah, but there's one thing I need to tell you," Melanie said, looking toward the ground.

"What is it?"

"Well, my sister doesn't believe in this stuff, so we can't tell her anything about you or Phineas. As of right now, this case is just about your cousin being accused of killing several people."

"Ok so no turning into a vampire around your sister- I think I can handle that," Evan said, wiping off some dirt from his jacket.

"She should be here by later tonight," Melanie said looking back around at the cemetery below.

They had decided to wait inside the manor until Melanie's sister got there before they would go and bail out Phineas. As they waited, they went over what they had seen at the moore and tried to piece together what could have happened. Since they couldn't figure out what could have happened, they moved onto Hayden and what he was trying to hide. As they were talking over points about Hayden, Evan started to talk about his family and brother.

"I had a brother for a short while," Evan said sitting at his dining room table.

"Really? Wait what do you mean "for a short while"," Melanie asked raising an eyebrow.

"He disappeared after a dispute with my folks," Evan paused, looking down at the table. "My parents said he was probably dead after a while of not hearing from him."

"What was the dispute about," Melanie asked looking at how bad Evan was hurting.

"He wanted to go to college and my parents said no, then when it was my turn to ask they said yes," Evan said looking down at the dining room table.

"So he thought they liked you better," Melanie said trying to understand his hurt.

"Yeah, but they were always trying to pull us apart," Evan said looking up at Melanie, "my parents would always treat me better and that made my brother jealous of me."

"Well maybe deep down your brother hated your parents and not you," Melanie said looking over at Evan.

"Maybe," Evan said, looking at her.

"Don't try anything buddy-I'm your cousin's girlfriend," Melanie said looking into Evan's blue eyes.

"I wasn't thinking about doing anything," he said looking away.

"Believe me, I know that look," Melanie said, chuckling under her breathe.

"No, believe me. You're human and I could never fall in love with a human," Evan said, as he walked away from the window.

"Why not?"

"Because I wouldn't want to have to go through the pain of watching a woman I love age and die without me. It couldn't work out and I am sure as hell not going to turn a woman into a creature like me just to live with her forever. That wouldn't be love, that would be a curse."

Silence fell over the two as what Evan just said soaked into the air. Melanie could understand his reasoning but she felt bad for him-having to be alone for the rest of his life. Melanie continued to look out the window when she saw something walking up the steps toward the manor.

"Ok, enough of the vampire talk," Melanie said, spinning around to look at Evan

"Why is that?"

"My sister is here," she said, as she walked toward the entry hall.

Melanie opened the door up, inviting in her sister, Stephanie. Stephanie took off her sun glasses and looked around. She was very breathtaking-with dark hair with a single purple stripe of hair in her bangs covering her one eye. Her wardrobe was a dark purple dress with a belt around the middle and high black boots. She looked like her sister, but more stunning with her brown eyes.

Evan couldn't help but notice her eyes and her beauty. This was the first time he had ever felt warm since he had been turned. He didn't know what had come over him, but he turned around and tried to shake the feeling. As he turned back around there was Melanie and her sister right in front of him. Melanie noticed the look in Evan's eyes as she introduced them.

"Evan, this is my sister Stephanie. Stephanie, this is Phineas's cousin Evan," she said pointing to each of them.

"Hello. Thank you for coming," Evan said, being the first to extend his hand.

"Hello, nice to meet you and no problem- I am always willing to help out with investigations," she said meeting his hand in the middle.

"So I think we might want to go and get Phineas now," Melanie said, interrupting their too-long hand shake.

"Yes, maybe we should do that," Evan said, letting go of Stephanie's hand.

"Ok, I'm going wherever you lead me," Stephanie said as she brushed her hair behind her ear, looking down at the ground with a smile on her face.

They called a cab to take them down to the police station. When the cab arrived they got in the back of the car, bunched together. When Evan discovered he was sitting so close to Stephanie, he decided to get out and sit in the front instead, giving the excuse that he was claustrophobic. Melanie gave him a strange look, but chose not to say anything about it.

As they came closer to the station where they were holding Phineas, the three of them discovered that this was a bigger deal than they had thought. News people were scattered in front of the station, talking to police and passersby. They got out of the cab and walked up the stairs, trying to avoid the media frenzy. Evan entered into the station first, and grabbed the first police officer he saw.

"Could you tell me where I can pay bail," Evan asked, looking at the cop.

"Right at that desk, against the wall there," the police office said, pointing to the oak desk that sat against the wall.

"Thanks."

Evan walked over to the desk and had to ring a bell for assistance. They waited for several minutes until someone finally came to the desk.

"May I help you sir," the clerk asked. She was a middle aged woman with her hair pulled back tightly, obviously unhappy to be there.

"Yes, I was wondering if I could bail my cousin out of jail," Evan said as he sat in the chair adjacent from the women.

"What's his name?"

"Phineas Daniels"

"Ok, let me go check and see if you can bail him out," she said, as she got up from her chair and walked into the office located to the right of her desk.

The minutes seemed to creep by as they waited for her to come back. Evan wondered what this would cost him. Just as Evan was about to talk to the girls the woman came back out and sat back down in front of them.

"To bail out your cousin, it's going to be $250, 000," she said as she wrote down some information on a piece of paper.

"Wow, really," Evan paused, thinking maybe Phineas was better off in jail. "Ok, here's the money."

The clerk was shocked to see so much cash. After taking a breath she continued, "Ok, I will get the papers ready for release." She went to go back in the office. When she returned she added, "I am going to have them release him in the back, so he doesn't have to put up with all that media."

"Thank you, we appreciate that," Evan said, standing up.

Again they waited for what felt like hours until the papers were ready to sign. Evan signed the papers without thinking that, if they did a background check, they wouldn't find him. As the woman took the papers back to file them, Evan turned back around to the girls.

"Maybe you guys should go ahead and have the cab pull around back and I will meet you out at the side."

"Ok, Stephanie, do you want to stay here with Evan while I go and have the cab move," Melanie asked, seeing the shocked look on Evan's face as she said it.

"Yeah, I can do that," Stephanie said, stepping closer to Evan.

"After we get back to the manor, we need to sit down and regroup before we follow any leads," Melanie said, as she turned to leave.

Evan became increasingly nervous waiting with Stephanie for the woman to come back. As they waited, Stephanie tried to make small talk but Evan couldn't follow it trying to keep his mind off of certain things. At last the woman came around the corner and handed copies of the papers to Evan, and told him that his cousin was being sent up to the back door. Evan turned to leave and ran smack into Stephanie and knocked her to the ground.

"I'm so sorry," Evan said kneeling down to make sure she was ok.

"That's alright, I shouldn't have been standing that close behind you," she said as she rubbed her head.

"Are you ok? Should we take you to a doctor," he asked, pulling her up from the ground.

"Nah, I will be alright, just a little bump that's all," she said keeping a hold of his hand.

"Well we better go then," Evan said still holding on to her hand as well, "they will be wondering where we are."

"Good point," she answered as she finally let go of his hand and they turned to leave.

They exited the station and saw the cab pulling up in the adjacent alley. They hurried down the stairs past the media to the cab. When they got in, Phineas was covering his face with a shirt Melanie had given him to make sure the media didn't see him.

"What took you so long," Phineas asked, pulling the shirt from his face as the cab pulled off.

"Well we had to wait long enough for them to post bail," Evan said turning toward Phineas, "You're lucky they even let you leave thinking that you killed all those people."

The cab driver looked back in the backseat and then turned around again nervously. They had decided to stop talking until they were in a safe place. As the cab pulled up in front of the estate they filed out of the car onto the sidewalk below the two houses. They walked in silence up to the manor hoping not to get any attention from within the estate.

"So have you guys found anything out while I was gone," Phineas said, sitting down at the dining room table.

"The only thing we found out was that your brother is acting pretty funny about all this," Evan said, sitting across from him, "He's the one that turned you in."

"I'm going to kill that asshole," Phineas said, looking out the window down at the estate.

"I thought you said he couldn't have murdered anybody? Now he is wanting to kill his own brother," Stephanie said, stepping closer to Evan's chair.

"He's just joking, he wouldn't really kill his brother," Melanie said as she stepped closer to Phineas's chair.

"How do you know what I would do," Phineas said, looking up at Melanie.

"Because I know you. Anyways, what are we going to do now?"

"Well, I think we need to talk to people close to Hayden, see if we can't find anything out about him," Evan said, looking up toward Melanie.

"Sounds like a good idea. Who would be a good person to talk to, Phineas?"

"Well we can talk to my sister, she lives in the house with him and his family," Phineas said, trying to think of who else they could talk to.

"Ok, do you know of anybody else," Melanie asked, noticing Phineas trying to think.

"I guess his wife would be another good lead to check out," Phineas said looking across to Evan.

"How about me and Phineas go talk to the sister and Stephanie, you and Evan can go talk to the wife," Melanie said, looking across to Stephanie and Evan. "Then we will meet back here and share what we found out."

Both groups left the manor and sought out their target person. Luckily for them, Hayden was away on business for the day and they could go into the estate without raising suspicion. Evan and Stephanie found the wife in the kitchen cooking dinner, while Phineas and Melanie found his sister upstairs in her room.

"Hello Mrs. Daniels," Evan started out, walking into the kitchen.

"Oh, hello. Evan isn't it," she said, wiping her hands off then extending it for a handshake.

"Yes," he said extending his hand, "and this is Stephanie, Melanie's sister."

"Hi," Stephanie said in a small voice.

"We were wondering if you have noticed any changes in your husband here lately," Evan asked, trying not to sound obvious.

"Well nothing major," she said trying to remember, "except that one day."

"Which day would that have been," Evan asked, looking intrigued.

"The day he went up to the manor about a couple of months before you moved in," she said as she tried to gather her thoughts, "he went up there and when he came back he was acting strange. He looked really pale and was going around the house looking at the pictures of the family. It was almost like he had amnesia."

"How's that?"

"He was asking me the names of our kids and his family. It was really strange he just walked around in a daze for the entire day. Then one night, he didn't come to bed, and his excuse was that he fell asleep in the den. Except he wasn't in there around three in the morning when I came down to check."

Evan and Stephanie exchanged glances not wanting to seem to suspicious. Evan decided to end the questioning and find out what Melanie and Phineas had discovered.

"Well, we will leave you to your dinner now," Evan said politely, excusing himself.

"Now that's definitely odd," Stephanie whispered into Evan's ear, as they turned to leave.

"Yes. Let's hope Phineas and Melanie have luck with his sister," Evan said, opening the front door for Stephanie.

Phineas and Melanie were just striking up conversation with Phineas's sister. After half-way through, Phineas finally got the courage to ask his sister about their brother, even though he looked at Melanie the whole time he asked the questions.

"Jennifer, I have to ask you something," Phineas began, "Have you noticed anything odd about Hayden lately?"

"Yeah, why? Have you noticed it too," Jennifer asked, looking between Phineas and Melanie.

"No, what have you noticed," Phineas said, perking up a bit.

"Well lately he has done nothing but sit in the den and watch out the window as if he is waiting on someone or something," she said, looking at Phineas.

"How's that odd," Phineas asked, looking confused.

"You know our brother. He always used to go out and work outside, or go to the bars, or hang out with friends-but now he is like a wall ornament. Just sits there all day staring out that window."

"When did you notice this," Phineas asked.

"It all started when he went up to the old manor one day. He went up there to clean the place up a bit and came back like he was a shell of a man."

"I think that's enough information for right now," Melanie interrupted, looking at Phineas.

"Thanks for talking with us Jen," Phineas said as they got up to leave.

"Anytime little bro," she said going back to her computer.

“We need to get back to the manor and see what Evan and Stephanie found out,” Melanie said, as they walked down the stairs.

“Yea, there is definitely something up with Hayden,” Phineas said, as they walked out the front door.

The two groups met up to exchange what they had discovered. Even though they knew something was up with Hayden, they couldn’t figure out what. Was someone putting him up to this? Was he under a spell of some sort? Or, had he seen something that had changed him?

Sadly they knew they couldn’t find out anything more because Hayden was now gone for a week on business. They were trying to decide their next move, but they couldn’t think of where to begin.

“I can go talk to my local contacts about,” Melanie paused and looked at Stephanie, “um… certain things.”

“I think that’s a good idea,” Evan said, looking over towards Melanie.

"Ok. Well, Phineas, you want to come with me and see what we can find out," Melanie asked turning towards him.

"Do I have a choice," Phineas asked with a smile.

"While you guys are doing that, Stephanie and I will look around in here to see what he might have seen to make him the way he is," Evan said, looking around.

"That's a good idea," Stephanie said, looking around as well, "Then, we will all meet back here and exchange info."

"Phineas, lets go," Melanie said, pulling on his coat collar.

"Hey, take it easy. This coat wasn't cheap ya know," Phineas said, quickly standing up.

"Oh stop crying and let's get a move on," she said, taking him by the hand and pulling him toward the front door.

As they left, Evan picked himself up from his chair and began to inspect the bookshelves that surrounded the den. Stephanie joined him but didn't really understand what they were looking for.

"So what exactly are we looking for," Stephanie asked, looking from the bookshelves to Evan across the room.

"I have no real clue," Evan said, as he continued to look, not taking his eyes from the shelves.

"Well that makes it easier," she said, as she rolled her eyes and turned back toward the bookshelves.

"Anything weird or out of place I guess would be the best thing to look for," Evan said, answering Stephanie's sarcasm.

"Evan, I have one question for you," Stephanie began, "You guys don't think any of this is supernatural do you?"

"Um, no. Not at all," he tried to find the words to say, "We just want to make sure we cover all angles to clear Phineas's name."

"I just wanted to make sure, because there's nothing supernatural about this," Stephanie said looking back at the bookshelves.

"I wouldn't be too sure about that," Evan whispered, turning to face the bookshelf in front of him.

"What was that," she asked, looking back around at him.

"Nothing," he said, with a bit of a grin on his face.

"Oh, ok," she said, again checking the shelves.

Evan and Stephanie continued to search the den, but found nothing. They moved on to other places in the house, but still couldn't find anything that would suggest a change in Hayden. The only place they had left to search was the basement.

Stephanie was resistant to enter into the creepy, cold basement. Evan took her hand and led her down the stairs with the lit candles in his other hand. In the light, the basement didn't look as eerie. The gray stone and floor looked like something out of a mad scientist's lab.

As they moved on, they began checking out all the cabinets and drawers. Stephanie came upon a spot in the wall she thought didn't look right. She began to feel around and noticed how the wall didn't meet up with the other side like it should.

"Evan, come over here I think I found something," She said as she continued to look at the wall.

"What is it," Evan asked, coming toward her looking concerned.

"I think I found a hidden door in the wall here," Stephanie answered back while looking back at him.

"Oh really," Evan said trying not to sound surprised by her discovery.

"Yeah, help me push it in," Stephanie said as Evan began pushing.

When they pushed on the wall, it gave and slid in about an inch. Knowing full well that he had to push the door aside he stood back looking puzzled so it would throw Stephanie off. Stephanie sat back and looked as well and finally Evan pushed the door aside and fell into the cavity making sure Stephanie knew he was never in there. Stephanie pulled out her flash light and shone it into the space. Then she let out a scream that even made Evan jump.

He jumped out of the space when he realized a body was lying against the floor, just near inches from where he was.

"Who is that," Stephanie asked, looking up at Evan.

"I think it's Hayden," he said, looking down at her.

"Is he dead," she asked, stepping back.

"I don't know, let me check," he said, getting closer to Hayden. After a pause, Evan put his hand on the side of Hayden's neck and felt a slight pulse.

"Well is he," Stephanie gulped, "dead."

“No, he is still alive,” Evan said picking him up, “I need to get him upstairs and lay him on the couch.”

Stephanie ascended the basement steps two at a time to grab the door for Evan. As they got upstairs, they made their way to the den where Evan placed his body on the sofa in front of the window.

“Should I call Melanie,” Stephanie asked, looking at Evan from behind.

“Yes, that might be a good idea,” he said, looking at her over his shoulder.

Chapter Nine

As the lead investigator in the gypsy's deaths, Nathan was sure he had got the right person. He had heard that they had let Phineas Daniels post bail, and he was aggravated about the whole situation. He was sitting behind his desk with his head in his hand trying to relax himself from the events that had occurred earlier in the day. As he was trying to relax, in walked a fellow investigator.

“Are you still upset that they let that Daniels boy post bail,” the investigator said, as he sat in the chair across from Nathan.

“Yeah, I’m pissed. We had key evidence proving he was the killer,” Nathan said, looking up at the investigator and then back down at his desk.

“Well as the saying goes, ‘everyone is innocent until proven guilty’,” the investigator said as he stood up to leave.

“Yeah, except when I know he is guilty that means he is guilty,” Nathan said, following the investigator with his eyes.

“Yeah whatever you say,” the investigator paused, taking a yellow envelope from his jacket, “By the way, a guy dropped this off to me to hand to you.”

“Who dropped it off? What’s in it,” Nathan asked, looking at the envelope.

“I don’t know the person. He just said to give it to you,” he said, as he walked out the door.

Nathan slowly opened the package, not knowing what was inside. He pulled out what appeared to be very old newspaper clippings. They were dated from back in the early 1900's. The headlines were about the great vampire attack on the fall festival, and the death of the Daniels family.

As he read on he came across a name he was very familiar with-Evan Daniels. Evan was mentioned several times-listed as missing and possibly dead. Nathan didn't understand until he flipped over to the next page. There, staring back from the page, was a picture of Evan Daniels-the person who was supposed to be missing. As he examined the picture, he noticed that the man staring back was the same man he had met earlier that day. He jumped up from his chair and ran to his office door. When he got into the hallway he yelled for one of the police officers.

"What's wrong," the officer said, looking concerned.

"I need you to look up everything you can on Evan Daniels," Nathan said looking at him intensely.

"Ok, why are you looking into him for," the officer asked, looking confused.

"Well, I just want some information on him," Nathan paused as he turned back toward his office.

Nathan went back into his office and closed the door. He was wondering how all this tied in with the murders of today. As he reread the newspaper article about the vampire attacks, he realized what this could possibly mean. Instead of Phineas being the guilty party, it might have been Phineas covering for his cousin.

He waited, with his head on his desk, for any news from the officer Just as Nathan was about to dose off, his door burst open and in walked the officer.

"Sorry to bust in like this sir," the officer said.

“No problem, what did you find out,” Nathan asked, listening intently.

“The only thing I could find on a Evan Daniels was from the early 1900’s. There’s absolutely nothing else. I called across the sea and they had no record of an Evan Daniels. It’s almost like he never existed, or at least not in this century,” the officer finished and sat down.

“That’s what I was afraid of,” Nathan said, looking from the news articles up to the officer. “Thanks for searching for me.”

“Not a problem sir,” the officer said as he got up, “But what does this mean exactly?”

“It means I might have to go and talk to Evan,” Nathan said, looking down toward his desk.

“You need any back up,” the officer asked.

“No, I think I can handle this on my own, but thanks anyways,” he said, as he started planning his next move.

Chapter Ten

Stephanie had stepped out to make the phone call to Melanie, as Evan stayed to take care of Hayden. Evan went and got water and opened up Hayden's mouth and made him drink it. Just from the water his heartbeat started to strengthen back to normal. It had almost appeared as if he had been starved for several days or possibly weeks. As Evan went back into the kitchen to find something more nutritious for him to eat, he heard Stephanie walk back in.

"They're on their way back now," Stephanie said, closing her cell phone.

"Ok. I gave him some water and I am trying to find something to feed him," Evan pause looking in the cabinet for food, "He almost looks like he has been starved."

"Yeah, he looks weak," Stephanie said, looking back toward the sofa.

"I don't understand how or why he was behind that wall though," Evan said, looking at Stephanie.

"I don't know either, unless he maybe got locked in by accident," she said, trying to think of an explanation.

Evan found something to feed to Hayden, as he was doing this, Stephanie stood behind him watching. He could feel Stephanie becoming more close to him and he was afraid of her intent toward him. It wasn't that he didn't feel the same way, but sadly he knew he couldn't feel the same way. The front door opened up and slammed as Melanie and Phineas came running in. They were shocked at what they saw on the sofa.

"What happened to him," Phineas asked, pointing toward his brother.

"We don't really know. We found him behind a secret hatch in the basement wall," Evan said, as he stood up.

"Is he able to speak," Melanie asked, looking between Evan and Stephanie.

"Not right now, he is very weak. It's almost as if he has been starved for several weeks," Evan answered back to Melanie.

"So what exactly does this mean," Phineas asked, looking at the three of them.

"I'm not quite sure, but hopefully he wakes up here shortly and then we can question him," Evan said as he looked back at Phineas.

"What's our next plan of attack," Melanie asked looking at Evan.

"Well I would like to talk to you guys alone outside for a few minutes," Evan answered in a whisper looking back at Stephanie.

"We will be right back," Melanie told her sister, who was sitting on a chair keeping an eye on Hayden.

"Ok, I'll watch him," Stephanie replied.

They all three stepped out onto the front porch, out of ear shot of Stephanie. Evan looked dazed as he was looking out over the cemetery below. Melanie and Phineas began to look at each other with worried looks on their faces.

"We know full well that he couldn't have been in that hatch for very long," Evan said as he continued to look over the cemetery.

"Yeah, because up till a couple of days ago you were in there," Phineas said coming closer to him.

"Yeah, so when did he get put in there," Melanie asked looking between Phineas and Evan.

"Remember the night we introduced myself to your brother," Evan asked turning back around to them, "I saw that shadow in the house and thought it was you."

"Yeah and I thought it was just your hunger talking," Phineas said pointing to him.

"What if there is a person acting like Hayden who had him locked up in one of the bedrooms here," Evan began looking back toward the cemetery, "then that night, knowing we were heading up here they came and moved him into that hatch."

"Wow, that would make explain so much," Melanie said with her hand under her chin thinking.

"I need to ask you guys a favor," Evan turned toward them with a serious look on his face.

"What is it," Melanie asked, looking up concerned.

"I need you two to go and ask Hayden's wife if she has heard from him lately," he said.

"What are you thinking," Phineas asked.

"I'm thinking that if she has then that will confirm our suspicions," Evan said walking back toward them.

"Then if we confirm this I can get in contact with some people who might know who this is we are dealing with," Melanie said nodding her head in reassurance.

"Then you and Stephanie can watch over Hayden then," Phineas asked looking at Evan.

"Yeah we will watch over Hayden," Evan answered back.

"Ok, we'll be right back," Melanie answered, pulling Phineas along.

Evan walked back into the house and took up a seat beside Stephanie. Stephanie looked up at Evan, wondering what was going on in that beautiful mind of his. She felt their connection growing stronger, and knew he had to have felt the same way about her as she did about him.

"So where did the rest of the team go," Stephanie asked, keeping her eyes on Evan.

"They are just going to check some things out for me," Evan answered, looking toward Stephanie and noticing her glistening eyes.

"Oh, ok," Stephanie answered back, still looking at Evan.

All of a sudden, Stephanie leaned in and gave Evan a kiss. Evan pulled back in surprise and didn't know what to say. Stephanie looked shocked at what Evan had done, and began to stand up clearly embarrassed.

"I'm sorry. I didn't mean to do that," Stephanie said, trying to hide the tears.

"Stephanie, I don't mean to be rude, but we can't do this," Evan said, stepping closer to her.

"Why not," Stephanie asked, seeming flabbergasted.

"I can't tell you why, you wouldn't understand," Evan answered back to her.

"It's ok. I get it," she said, turning around and heading toward the stairs.

"No, wait," Evan answered back in a whisper. It hadn't mattered it fell onto deaf ears, because Stephanie was already up the stairs and out of earshot.

Evan started to pace the den's floor thinking about what just had happened. He did find her attractive, but because he was what he was he couldn't have any kind of relationship, let alone fall in love with her. As it continued to eat away at him, he heard the front door open and thought it to be Melanie and Phineas.

"So what did you find out," Evan said, turning the corner to the front entrance.

"Oh, I am sorry Mr. Daniels, were you expecting someone else," Nathan asked, as he walked farther into the entrance way with a pistol aimed at Evan.

"What the hell do you think you are doing," Evan said, sounding heated.

"Well I got some interesting news articles today about who you really are, Mr. Daniels," he said with a slight grin.

“I am sure I don’t know what you mean,” Evan answered, back looking worried.

“Oh I think you do”, Nathan paused, “You’re a vampire and you killed those people in the woods and you let your cousin take the blame for it.”

“For one, I didn’t kill anyone, and two, you’re right-I am a vampire and you made a bad move coming here all alone,” Evan said as he turned.

“I think I can handle you,” Nathan said, not budging a bit.

“Evan,” Stephanie’s voice drifted from the top of the steps as she descended.

Evan looked up over his shoulder and saw Stephanie coming down the stairs. Stephanie saw Evan’s eyes and fangs and started to scream. Doing this caused Nathan to jump, and as he did, the gun went off hitting Stephanie in the chest. She tumbled down the stairs and landed in a heap on the floor below.

“You asshole! You killed her,” Evan screamed at Nathan.

“She will be in my report as just another casualty of yours,” Nathan answered back to Evan.

“You’re a dead man,” Evan said as he lunged toward Nathan.

Nathan started to fire rounds into Evan, but to no avail. Evan came closer and closer to Nathan. He knew that the gun was not going to work, but he kept using it anyway, hoping he would get the kill shot. By time he was out of bullets, Evan was right in front of him, laughing at the horrible mistake he was making.

Evan, instead of ripping out Nathan’s throat, decided to go for a more practical approach. He punched his hand into Nathan’s chest creating a hole. He pushed deeper in and clutched his heart and ripped it out. Nathan’s face went from terror to completely emotionless. After Nathan’s body dropped to the floor, Evan ran to Stephanie’s side. He could feel a slight heart beat but it was fading fast. Just as he made this discovery, Phineas and Melanie walked in.

"What happened," asked Phineas, as he only noticed the investigator's body in front of the door.

"STEPHANIE," Melanie screamed, as she came running into the entrance way, shoving Phineas out of the way.

"The investigator found out what I am and tried to shoot me, but Stephanie came down the stairs and he shot her first," Evan hurriedly explained.

"Is she dead," Melanie asked, holding on to her little sister.

"She has a slight heart beat, but it's fading fast," Evan answered, walking over toward Phineas trying not to get choked up.

"Turn her," Melanie said, looking at Evan through tear-soaked eyes.

"I can't do that! I couldn't let her live with the curse I have," Evan shot back.

"You have to, that's the only way we can save her," Melanie said, sobbing.

"It wouldn't be saving her, it would be cursing her," Evan paused, "I couldn't do that."

"Man, just do it for Melanie's sake," Phineas said, turning toward Evan shoulder to shoulder, "and yours."

"If I do this," Evan paused running his hand through his hair, "I am going to have to help her control her urges to feed off all of you. Phineas, while I am doing this, go and find me some small animals, like a deer or rabbit or something, and meet us in the family crypt."

"Ok, I'll do that," Phineas answered, running back out the door.

"Melanie, look away. I don't want you to see what I am going to do," Evan said as he knelt beside Stephanie's body.

Melanie moved away and walked into the den, facing opposite the scene from behind. Evan turned and sank his teeth into Stephanie's neck and started to drink some of the blood. He pulled away after just a second of draining her blood, hoping this would work. He had never changed somebody before, and he was just going on what had happened to himself.

He felt her drift away as he did the night he was turned. He picked her up and carried her to the basement door, where Melanie opened the door and followed them downstairs. As they got into the tunnel, it was extremely hard for Melanie to see but Evan could see perfectly.

"So what will happen now," Melanie asked, still crying.

"Well, I am going to have to lock her in the crypt and help her control her urges to feed off of you and Phineas," Evan answered, as he began walking faster.

"How long will that take," Melanie asked.

"Well for me, it took three years to get over my urges, but I am hoping with my help it will take a day or two," he said.

"I hope it doesn't take that long," Melanie said, starting to cry again.

As they entered the basement, Phineas was on the other side waiting for them. On the middle slab in the crypt laid two big deer freshly killed. Evan laid Stephanie down in the exact same corner he was in when had locked himself in. He walked out of the crypt and approached Phineas and Melanie.

"Listen, I need you guys to lock us in there and bring small animals every once in a while," Evan paused running his hand through his hair, "When she wakes up she is going to be really hungry, and I can't guarantee she won't try to kill me in an attempt to escape, so just be warned."

"I will make sure I bring in enough food for her," Phineas said, looking at Evan.

Evan nodded to this and went back into the crypt. Phineas latched the door and put the lock on to help keep them in. As he did that, Melanie sat on his bed and began to cry uncontrollable. Phineas came over to her, wrapped his arm around her and she laid her head on his shoulders.

"Do you think I did the right thing by telling Evan to turn her," Melanie asked, looking up at Phineas through tear soaked eyes.

"I think you made the hardest decision anyone has ever had to make," Phineas paused looking for the right words, "and if Evan does a good job, which I know he will, you will have your sister back without any harm. I mean, look at Evan. He lives a normal life-somewhat normal anyway."

"I guess your right," Melanie said, still looking worried. "I just hope everything turns out for the best."

Chapter Eleven

Evan was sitting in the opposite corner from Stephanie waiting for the moment when her eyes would shoot open. As he waited, he went over in his head what he would tell her. Now he could tell her the real reason why he couldn't love her before but now he could love her, if she wasn't too mad at him. As he was thinking about that he noticed out of the corner of his eyes Stephanie's body twitched.

He stood up and walked over to her, he sat behind her body and pulled her closer to him. Right as he did that her eyes shot open with blood shot eyes and then her whole body started to twitch and convulse just like Evan's body did that night so many years ago. Evan held onto her body and tried to control her involuntary muscles movements. It was when her muscles tensed up and then her whole body slumped against his that he knew she had turned.

He jumped up and held on to her tightly. He escorted her over to the deer sitting on the concrete slap. Stephanie looked down at the deer and back up at Evan. She understood what he wanted her to do, so she began to tear into the deer and feed on its blood. After she got past the first deer, she began on the second one. Luckily, she only made it half way through before her hunger subsided. She went back to the corner and tried to put together what had happened to her. She looked up at Evan every once in a while, and still couldn't understand everything that had happened.

"I'm sure you want to know what happened to you," Evan finally broke the silence.

"All I remember is I came down the stairs and saw your face, and next thing I remember was getting shot," Stephanie said in a hushed tone.

"Yes, that psychotic investigator shot and killed you," Evan paused, "then your sister came in and asked me to turn you so you wouldn't die. I had no choice. I didn't want to see you die either, but I also didn't want to give you my curse."

"Wait, is this the reason you wouldn't kiss me," Stephanie asked, looking up at Evan.

"Yes. I could never take the risk of falling in love. I didn't want to be with someone I had to watch age and die without me," Evan answered back.

"So are you saying things are different now," she asked.

"If it's still something you want to explore," Evan said, looking down toward the ground.

"Yeah…I mean, I understand about you not wanting to give me your curse, but by doing so you saved my life. And, who knows, perhaps you have given us a chance at a life together," she said as she slowly got up and hugged Evan. "So when can I see my sister again?"

"Well hopefully in a couple days," Evan answered.

"Why a couple days and not now," she said, cocking her head to the left.

"Because we need to get this hunger of yours under control before you see your sister. If we don't work on that, you might end up killing people. Believe me, once the hunger takes control, you can kill your loved ones without a second thought. Sadly, I know from experience."

"Why, what happened," Stephanie asked.

"When I was turned about a hundred years ago, my hunger was so overwhelming I came back to my house, where Hayden's family now lives, and killed my father, mother and our maid when I finally realized what was happening, it was too late."

"Evan," Stephanie said feeling his pain, "Please help me control this hunger I don't want to kill people."

"That's why I had Phineas lock us in my family crypt," Evan said, "This is where I came after I killed my family and I hid out in here and waited for my hunger to get under control. Don't worry, I will help you control your urges."

"Thank you," Stephanie said, as she hugged Evan tightly.

Chapter Twelve

Phineas and Melanie heard the conversation going on inside the crypt. Melanie was pleased to hear her sister's voice again. This calmed her, and she fell asleep in Phineas arms.

After a short while, Phineas slowly laid his girlfriend down on his bed and went to go through the tunnel to check on Hayden. He entered into the dark tunnel and put his hand on the wall as he walked deeper in. The wall was cold and moist. As he finally came to the doors he entered the manor.

Once inside, he found his way to the stairs and made his way up to the first floor. When he approached his brother's body on the sofa, he noticed his chest rising and falling. As he stood over his brother, he didn't know if it would be a good idea to try and wake him or not. Pacing as he debated what to do, he hadn't realized his brother was already awake watching him pace back and forth.

"What are you doing, Phineas," he said in a hushed tone, causing Phineas to jump.

"Hey you're awake," Phineas said, trying to hide his shock, "I was scared there for a bit that you wouldn't wake up."

"What happened to me," Hayden asked, sitting up, "Where am I?"

"What do you remember," Phineas asked, planting himself in a chair across from him.

"Well, the last thing I remember is that I was going up to clean the manor and next thing I know I was knocked out cold," he said, rubbing the back of his head.

"Well, when exactly did you come up here," Phineas asked looking more interested.

"It was middle of August," Hayden answered looking up at Phineas, "Why? How long have I been out?"

"Um, it's the end of October big bro," Phineas said, standing up from his chair.

"It can't be! I mean, it was just August! How did two months pass without me knowing," Hayden asked, in complete shock at what he was hearing.

"Well it is, and I am not sure how exactly this happened, but I think we need to go talk with Melanie," Phineas said, grabbing his brothers arm and pulling him along.

"Ok, ok-take it easy on my arm, it's attached you know," Hayden said, trying to pull his arm free.

Phineas let go of his brother's arm and led him down into the basement. They walked over to the tunnel entrance. As Phineas began, he again put his hand against the wall for guidance and his brother did the same.

To Hayden, it seemed like the tunnel dragged on and on, but for Phineas, he knew that the end was coming closer. The small sliver of light coming from the basement was coming into view as they continued to walk. As Phineas walked into the basement, there was his girlfriend still asleep on his bed curled up in his blanket. He walked over to the bed and sat on the edge and combed his hand through her hair. Her beauty was mystical, even to Phineas. She slowly opened her eyes and looked up at him.

"Hi babe, we need to ask you a few questions," Phineas said in a whispered tone.

"Who is *we*," Melanie said, whispering back.

"Me and Hayden," he turned and pointed, "He finally woke up.

"Oh ok," Melanie said, pushing her self up, "What's the questions?"

"Well Hayden said back in August he was attacked at the manor, and he doesn't remember anything after that," Phineas said looking down at her, "So I think we are looking at a person who is impersonating Hayden."

"We figured that out after talking to Hayden's wife," Melanie answered back, wiping the sleep out of her eyes.

"I know, but I just wanted to make sure of it," Phineas said, looking back at Hayden.

"Wait-you guys know what's happening to me and you haven't told me," Hayden asked, looking peeved.

"Well, I needed Melanie to assure my thoughts before I told you anything," Phineas answered.

"We think there is a doppelganger of you out there," Melanie paused, looking away.

"Is there something else, Melanie," Hayden asked.

"There might be a small chance we're not dealing with a doppelganger, but a shape-shifter instead," she answered, looking up shamefully.

"And what in the hell is a shape-shifter," Phineas said, standing up straight.

"It's a person that can change into other people, taking on their personality and everything," Melanie answered, looking to Phineas.

"Is that even possible," Hayden asked, "I mean, that's not real is it?"

"Well, a lot of things are real that I am sure you don't think are," she said, looking up at him.

"Like what exactly," he inquired looking at Phineas.

"There are two things I need to tell you, Hayden," Phineas paused and then, with the help of the ring, turned into a werewolf, "See, there are certain things that might not seem real but are. And by the way, we have a vampire cousin who is a hundred years old with a newly turned vamp locked in the crypt."

"Holy Shit," Hayden said as he jumped back against the wall and coward in fear.

"Don't worry as long as I have this ring on I can't hurt you," Phineas said, turning back into his human form.

"So, do you believe us now," Melanie asked, watching Hayden's panic-stricken face relax.

"Yeah, I believe you now," he said, breathing so hard he could barely speak, "But how do we get rid of this shape-shifter?"

"Well, that's the hard part," Melanie said, standing up beside Phineas, "It's hard to find a shape-shifter since they can blend in with everyone else."

"So you're saying anyone of us can be a shape-shifter right now and not even know it," Hayden said, looking shocked.

"Yeah, except since we are trying to find the shape-shifter I don't think we have to worry about it, because the shifter would want to detour us from looking not attract us to looking," Melanie said, looking between Phineas and Hayden.

"What do we do now," Hayden said, looking at the two of them.

"I think you need to stay up in the manor. When the fake Hayden comes back, we will set the trap," Melanie paused, looking toward the crypt, "We should wait until they are finished before we plan our next big move."

"How long are they going to be," Hayden asked, pointing toward the door.

"Well Evan is trying to get Stephanie's urges under control so she can help us continue the search, it shouldn't take more than a couple days," Phineas said, looking from the crypt to Hayden.

"A couple days. What if the shifter shows up and tries to kill my family," Hayden said, looking worried.

“We will keep an eye out on the house and, if we see him, then we will go down there and confront him… and possibly kill him,” Phineas answered back.

“Ok… sounds like a plan,” Hayden said.

They all decided to hangout in the basement for a while and catch up with each other. Phineas began to tell Hayden about their vampire cousin. As he listened, Hayden still had trouble believing it. He didn’t understand how, everything he thought was just a work of fiction, was actually true.

The catch-up session was coming to an end when a loud knock came from the crypt. All three of them turned their heads to the door startled by the sound. Phineas slowly got up, went to the door and placed his ear against it.

“Evan, is that you,” Phineas said, whispering to the door.

“Yes, it’s me,” Evan answered back through the door.

"How is it going in there," Phineas asked, looking back toward Hayden and Melanie.

"It's going good. She understands what I did, and she really wants to see Melanie," Evan answered back.

"That's a good thing," Phineas said, still looking at Melanie and noticing tears forming in her eyes.

"I need a few more small animals for when she wakes up again," Evan whispered.

"Ok, I will go and get some right now," Phineas said pausing, "Hayden's awake now and our fears are true-there is someone out there trying to be him, trying to live his life."

"I figured that," Evan said with a pause, "Listen, I think we will be good to get out in another day or so. When I get out of here we will figure out a plan of attack."

"Is there anything else you need before I leave," Phineas asked.

"No, just some small animals. Bring more than before, because I am going to have to feed as well," Evan responded.

"Ok, I'll be back soon. If you need anything else, Melanie and Hayden are out here," Phineas said as he went to walk away.

"Ok, I'm sure we'll be fine," Evan said as his voice became more distant.

Phineas walked off through the tunnel to collect more animals and Hayden had decided to go back up to the manor and get cleaned up. Melanie stayed in the basement in case Evan and Stephanie needed anything. She was glad to have some alone time to relax and breath… time to let everything sink in. She briefly thought about how they would handle the shape shifter situation before she slowly drifted back to sleep on Phineas's bed.

Phineas was just reaching the doors that would lead out to the Moore. As he opened up the door in the side of the hill, he noticed the moon was bright, lighting up the entire Moore.

He was happy that it wasn't quite yet the full moon. He descended down the hill, his tracking senses coming into use. He heard several animals in the woods, but couldn't quite figure out in which direction the animals were located. He decided to turn into a wolf so he could track better.

As a wolf, his senses made it easy to track several deer down and subdue the creatures. He tracked down several other animals as well, and stockpiled them at the edge of the Moore. After a few more animals, he figured that would last them for a short while. He tried his best to drag all the animals up the hill but couldn't get them all in one pass. He took the deer up to the door first and then went down for the smaller animals second. By the time he had tracked, killed, and moved the animals, he noticed the sun was slowly rising in the eastern sky. He hadn't realized how long it had taken him to do the task.

He finally got the animals to the basement and discovered Melanie out cold on his bed again. He pulled the animals to the crypt door and knocked lightly hoping not to disturb Stephanie.

"Phineas," Evan's voice whispered.

"Yeah, I have several animals for you," Phineas said trying to get the animals closer to the door.

"Ok, unlock the door and I will take them one at a time," Evan answered back.

Phineas unlocked the door slowly and quietly started to hand the animals to Evan one by one. Evan was shocked at how many animals he had collected. After the last animal went through the door, Evan made a motion to hurry and shut the door. Phineas saw Stephanie start to stir over against wall and got the hint. He closed the door lightly and locked it back hoping to not wake Melanie. After he finished, he walked over toward his bed and laid down behind Melanie. He cuddled up to her and laid his arm over her body. She, in turn, laid her hand on his. Phineas pulled the blanket over the two of them and then slowly fell asleep.

Chapter Thirteen

Hayden lowered himself into the bath. The warm water felt good, and he laid his head back against the tubs rim. He had to try and relax and take in everything he had heard that night. As he relaxed, he slowly fell asleep. Luckily his feet reached the other end of the tub, therefore keeping him above the water while he dosed off.

He awoke about an hour later and found the water was now cold. He slowly stood up and began to dry himself off. After he was dried, he wrapped the towel around his lower waist and walked out of the bathroom and explored the house, hoping to find some clothes to wear. He stumbled into Evan's room and found his new batch of clothes in the closet. He looked through his wardrobe and found a nice dress shirt and pants to wear. He threw them on, and began making his way through the manor.

He couldn't believe all of the amazing things that were stored in the manor. If he had known all the great things that were located in the manor he would have moved into the manor himself instead of the estate. He found his way to the kitchen and looked through the cabinets for food, only finding crackers and soup. Deciding this would be enough for him, he lit the stove and began to cook his breakfast.

After the soup was done, he sat in the den and ate it quietly, watching over his house below. The sun had already risen and the shadows were crawling down the hill from his house. He noticed that the leaves had started to fall from the trees and he remembered that Phineas told him it was the end of October. He still couldn't believe what had happened to him. Unfortunately that wasn't the only weird thing that had happened to Hayden.

Hayden had noticed, years before, that he could move things, do things, just by thinking about it. He couldn't remember what it was called exactly, but at first he was terrified of it. That was until he learned to control his mind and channel his thoughts carefully. It seemed, with Phineas being a Werewolf and Evan being a hundred year old vampire, that the Daniels family had a curse on them. Hayden didn't know how or why, but it just seemed that the family was cursed.

Hayden had finished his soup and got up to go back through the tunnel to the basement of the estate. He made his way closer to the basement and noticed the light coming from within the room. As he entered the room, he saw Phineas and Melanie were both asleep on

Phineas's bed. He looked around and found an extra pillow and blanket against the wall, and decided to take them and lay down on the concrete floor. It wasn't very comfortable, but he had a feeling he wouldn't be asleep long.

Chapter Fourteen

On the second full day of being locked in the crypt Evan was still working with Stephanie on how to control her urges. She had come a far way, a lot better than Evan had done when he was locked in the crypt. Then again, Evan had to credit this to him being there to help her through the transformation.

As the second day was ending Stephanie and Evan had fallen asleep together in the one corner of the crypt. Evan was awake and watched as Stephanie slept in his arms. He was thinking about how his feelings for her had grown-he had only met her about three days before. Maybe it was because she now shared this curse with him, and she could understand him in ways no one else could. But he couldn't let go of this feeling that, maybe, he had found someone to share his life, or "unlife" with. He slowly drifted asleep with this thought in mind.

They had slept there together for several hours before Evan was awaken by Stephanie kissing his cheek. Evan looked down at her, and she up at him. Stephanie began to kiss him. After a few seconds, she pulled back and sat up on her side looking down at Evan.

"I feel this connection with you," Stephanie said.

"I know what you mean. I feel it too," Evan replied, shyly smiling at her.

“Why is that? Do you think it’s just because we share this, you know, ‘curse’, or is it something more,” asked Stephanie.

“Perhaps both,” Evan said, still smiling.

“I’d like to think so,” said Stephanie, leaning in to kiss him again.

Stephanie then laid back down in Evan’s arms with her head on his chest. She giggled to herself when she realized there was no heartbeat to hear. So she just closed her eyes, thinking about what she had experienced over the past few days, and what still lay ahead.

****

Outside in the basement of the estate the time past more slowly than what it seemed to in the crypt. As the days passed the group had to find other things to do to keep themselves busy or occupied. Most of the time they would play cards or other board games while they waited or just talked about each of their lives.

They each would take turns going up to the manor and watching the estate below, making sure that the Hayden look-a-like didn't come back. On the first watch up in the manor they decided to clean up the mess that had been left behind from Evan's kill. Phineas took the body of the investigator and threw him into a crypt that was in the older part of the cemetery. Luckily for them, no one came to check and see if the investigator had been up to the manor.

****

The third day came and went without any sightings of the other Hayden. As the third day came to a close Hayden, Melanie and Phineas all met back at the basement of the estate. Just as Hayden was getting ready to take his post up in the manor, a loud bang came from with in the crypt. They all turned and stared waiting for a reply.

"Phineas, I think we're ready to come out now," Evan's voice echoed through the silent basement.

"Ok," Phineas answered back, running up to the door to unlock it.

Phineas broke the lock off the door and slowly pulled it open. There, standing in the doorway, was Evan and Stephanie. Stephanie came running toward Melanie with her arms wide open. Evan was along side her to make sure her first contact with Melanie didn't end badly.

As they embraced Evan watched Stephanie's face very closely and was shocked the temptation from her sister hadn't made her try and bite her. A second later they pulled themselves apart and turned around to join the rest of the group.

"I can't believe you weren't even tempted to bite your sister's neck," Evan said, still surprised by Stephanie's restraint.

"Well, what can I say, I had a good teacher," Stephanie said, closing the gap between her and Evan.

"Maybe it's because your first meal wasn't human blood. Maybe that's why you weren't tempted," Evan said, looking at Stephanie.

"Maybe it was or maybe it wasn't, who knows," Stephanie said, grabbing ahold of his arm.

"So, now that you are out, I would like to introduce you to my real brother. Hayden, this is Evan, Evan this is Hayden," Phineas said, pointing to each of them.

"Hello, nice to meet the real Hayden," Evan said reaching out a hand.

"Nice to meet you as well," Hayden said returning the gesture.

"Now that we have got past that, we need to figure out what we are going to do next," Melanie said, looking at the four of them.

"Yeah, what are we going to do with the person who is pretending to be me," Hayden asked.

"All in good time," Evan responded.

"All in good time my ass! Every minute we wait is putting my family at risk," Hayden said, getting angry.

"We wait until we get up in the manor before we make any plans," Evan said, getting in Hayden's face, "because he might be listening in on us right now and we wouldn't even know it."

They all made their way up the dark tunnel toward the manor. The silence was deafening in the tunnel and the cold air made it even creepier. They finally came to the basement of the manor and stopped. Evan rushed them into the basement and slammed the door behind them. He then took his place at the head of the line and led them upstairs to the den. Each one of them taking their seats around the room as Evan stood by the fireplace.

"Melanie, do you have any contacts that might know about shape-shifters," Evan asked, looking into the fireplace.

"There is this one guy who might know."

"I say you should find out if he might know anything and see if he has any ideas where this other Hayden might be," Evan answered back looking up from the fireplace to Melanie.

"I could do that. It might take a while to track the guy down, but by the end of the day I should be able to find him," Melanie said, looking from Evan to the window.

"Ok, I think that's the first step we should take," Evan said as he looked back to the rest of the group.

"What are the rest of us going to do," Hayden said looking at Evan.

"Well you should try to stay out of sight, and Stephanie and I will go and research some things at the newspaper office," Evan said, looking at Stephanie.

"What will you find out there," Hayden asked, sounding annoyed.

"I am hoping to see if anyone has went missing in the past couple of months, if there has, that person might be the shape-shifter," Evan answered looking toward Hayden.

"I have an idea, Evan," Melanie said looking up at him, "How about Phineas goes with Stephanie and does research, and I will go on my own and you stay here with Hayden? Then we make sure the other Hayden doesn't come back and try and kill the real Hayden."

"That's a good point," Evan said, looking down at the floor and rubbing his chin, "Phineas you call me though if anything happens with Stephanie."

"I am sure I can handle her," Phineas said, looking from Stephanie to Evan.

"I meant if she goes to turn, call me. She has only been out, what, a half an hour," Evan said looking at Stephanie.

"Hey, I think I will be fine. I know how to control the urges," Stephanie said looking up at Evan.

"I know, I just don't want anything to happen to you," Evan said, looking concerned.

"I'll be ok," Stephanie said, still looking up at him.

"Gees, why don't you two get a room," Phineas said, looking at the both of them.

“Shut up,” Melanie said, slapping him in the back of the head.

“Ouch, what was that for,” Phineas asked rubbing his head.

“Seriously, you can’t figure it out,” Melanie answered back in a sarcastic tone.

Melanie got up and left as did Phineas and Stephanie. Stephanie hugged Evan before leaving and assured him she would be fine. When everyone left Hayden decided to go upstairs and lie down until the others got back with some news. Evan waited in the den, when he heard the front door open up and close. He stood up to see who it was and was surprised to see it was Stephanie.

“Hey what are you doing back so soon,” Evan asked looking at her.

“I forgot something,” Stephanie answered with a quick response.

“Oh what did you forget,” he said looking at her with compassion.

"Um, I can't seem to remember," she said looking up at him.

"Ok, that solves it, you stay here," Evan said with a grin.

"Oh, now I remember… when exactly did Hayden start acting funny," she said, looking down at the ground then back up to him.

"Well, his wife said he started acting funny about a couple of months before I arrived, so that would put it around August I guess," he answered, "Why do you need to know that?"

"So I can have a reference point to start checking," she answered, "Well, I am off again."

"Aren't you forgetting something," Evan asked.

"What is that," she said, not seeming to understand.

"This," Evan answered, pulling her close and kissing her.

She quickly pulled back, stunned, and ran out the door. Evan was shocked by her response and didn't know what had gotten into her. He decided to leave it at that until later when he could talk to her by himself.

Chapter Fifteen

When Melanie left the manor, she had no real clue where to find the guy she was looking for. She wasn't even sure if he was in the same state, he could be any where in the world at this time. She was hoping, by luck, he would be some where close. As she walked down the street, she found the shop she was looking for.

She darted inside and began to look around. The shelves were covered in magical items and supernatural treasures. She got closer to the counter where a very beautiful girl was standing, trying to stock shelves. The girl was dressed in all black and had long black hair with strips of blond highlights. As Melanie came closer, she recognized the girl.

"Emma," Melanie said, trying not to startle the girl.

"Melanie," the girl said, turning to meet her.

"Yeah, it's me," Melanie answered, as Emma came over and hugged her.

"It's been so long," Emma said looking at Melanie.

"Yes it has been," Melanie said, looking down at the floor.

"What's wrong," Emma asked.

"I wish this was just a social call but I need help finding someone," Melanie said looking up at Emma.

"Hey no problem, maybe we can have a social call some other time," Emma said putting her hand on Melanie's shoulder, "So who is it you have to find."

"I need to find Lucas and see what he can tell me about local shape-shifters," Melanie answered.

"Well, I don't know where he is personally, but I know a girl you can call to find out," Emma paused, looking toward the back of her store then back to Melanie, "Do you want her number."

"Yeah I'll take her number. I need to find him fast," Melanie said.

"Ok, let me go in the back and find her number," Emma said.

Emma walked toward the back of the store to retrieve the number leaving Melanie in the store room by herself. Melanie began to look at the different things in the shop. There were herbs and spices and black magic stuff that Melanie herself wouldn't even think about touching. As Melanie continued looking around she came across something that made her chuckle. In front of her on a lower shelf was a vampire hunter kit. The kit included a case with holy water and two stakes. She thought about buying it as a gag gift for Evan and Stephanie, but her thought was interrupted by Emma reentering the store room. As she came around the counter she saw Emma carrying a business card in her one hand.

"Here's her number," Emma said handing over the card to Melanie.

"I appreciate this so much."

"Hey, just remember after you find this guy and sort things out, call me so we can hang out sometime," Emma replied.

"Don't worry, I definitely will," Melanie said as she headed out the door.

Melanie couldn't wait to get away from people before she made the call. Just a few steps out of the shop, she was reaching for her phone. She looked at the card and dialed the number into her phone and pressed send. Ringing came from the other line and then, within seconds, someone picked up.

“Hello, can I help,” a voice answered.

“Yes, is this Allison,” Melanie asked, waiting for an answer.

“Yeah this is her, who is this,” Allison asked.

“This is Melanie, a friend of Emma’s. She said I should call you to find Lucas,” Melanie said.

“I think I can help you with that, give me a second,” Allison said, then leaving the phone silent for several seconds. “Lucas is in the U.S., the Midwest actually.”

“Great that’s where I am,” Melanie answered back.

“You’re in luck,” Allison said,” I am going to track your cell phone to get your coordinates and send him a message.” There was silence as Allison tracked Melanie’s phone, then she continued, “Huh, what do ya know! He’s very close in fact, he’ll be there within minutes.”

“Oh my god, that’s amazing,” Melanie answered, pausing outside a café. She decided to wait there for him.

“I have collected the info and sent it to him. Don’t move-he should be there in a matter of minutes,” Allison said.

“Great, thanks for your help Allison.”

“No problem-hope Lucas can help,” replied Allison. And with that, the call was over.

Melanie closed her phone and found a table to sit at in the café. Before she could even sit down, Lucas suddenly appeared before her. She was taken back by this, and looked around to see if anybody else had noticed what she had just witnessed. Lucas looked up at her through sunglasses and smiled. She walked over to the table and sat down.

“Lucas,” Melanie said, looking at him.

“Who else would I be,” Lucas said with a big grin on his face.

"Ok, I don't have time to socialize, so down to business. I need help finding a shape-shifter," Melanie said, whispering the last part.

"I already knew that," Lucas said, still grinning.

"So, have you found any in this area," Melanie asked, slightly annoyed.

"I have found one, but most likely he is dead. There hasn't been any activity on him since about 1910," Lucas said, lowering his sunglasses and revealing bright blue eyes.

"Who is the one from 1910," Melanie asked, looking more interested.

"Somebody by the name of Adam Daniels," Lucas said, pushing his glasses back up.

"You have got to be kidding me," Melanie said, sitting back in her chair.

"What? Do you know him," Lucas asked.

"Let's just say I might know his relative," Melanie said, shaking her head at what she had just learned.

"Are you talking about Evan Daniels," he said, pausing and then looking around the café, "Rumor has it he has resurfaced."

"How do you know about Evan," Melanie asked.

"I know about everything and everybody in the supernatural world," Lucas replied.

"Then I can tell you he has resurfaced. I am helping him and his cousins through some things," Melanie said whispering.

"Well, if you guys need anything from me you know where to reach me," Lucas said, looking more serious, "but be careful because there is some turbulence within the vampire and werewolf clans about how close Phineas and Evan are."

"What's so bad about them being close," she asked, looking confused.

"You should know, vampires and werewolfs are supposed to be enemies and when two become family members, let alone good friends… well, lets just say it might end in a messy situation," Lucas said, standing up from the table.

"I will be sure to let them know."

"Like I said, if you need me again, you know how to get a hold of me," he said, looking down at her.

"Ok, thanks again for the info, Lucas," Melanie said looking from the table to where Lucas was, but surprised to find the space empty.

Melanie got up from the table, went up to the counter and ordered five hot chocolates- thinking that the group might need them. She walked out of the café and began to head back to the manor. She noticed that the air had gotten cooler and the sun was about to set. She hurried her pace so she could get back up to the manor. As she walked past the estate, she noticed that all the lights were on in the house. Not thinking it was a big deal, she continued up the hill with the hot chocolate.

Chapter Sixteen

Phineas and Stephanie walked downtown, not wanting to call for a cab. As they walked, they both were enjoying the fall air as it had a different scent to it than any other season. Stephanie had just noticed the sun shining on her and was shocked.

"I am taking it the whole vampire in sunlight thing is just a myth," Stephanie said, looking down at her skin.

"Yeah, I think it is," Phineas said looking at her, "If it were true, you would be dead by now, and so would Evan."

"That's true, I keep forgetting about Evan being more used to this than me," she said, looking up to Phineas.

"Yeah being a hundred years old has some benefits I suppose," Phineas said laughing.

"I guess your right," Stephanie said with a smile.

They arrived at the newspaper office and found the two months worth of newspapers. They each took a roll of the film and began to search for any missing persons they could find, but nothing was turning up.

"I think this is a bust," Phineas said, turning around to look at Stephanie.

"Just keep looking," Stephanie said, rolling her eyes at him.

"Wait-I think I found something," Phineas said.

"What is it?"

"It's a girl who disappeared about two months ago, right around the time Hayden changed," Phineas said, looking up at Stephanie.

"Yeah but one problem Phineas," she said stifling a laugh, "this girl was six years old."

"Yeah, so what does that mean? Six year olds can't be shape-shifters," he said, looking annoyed.

"Well, I thought I had heard Melanie say something like shape-shifters can't start changing into things until their teenage years," Stephanie said, sliding back over to her computer.

"So what, this is the best I can do," Phineas said, turning back to his computer.

"I swear, you have no patience," Stephanie said, letting out a little chuckle.

"Hey, you try looking at this boring stuff while having A.D.D.," he said, continuing to look.

The search didn't turn out as they had hoped. They left the newspaper office after just being there an hour. While walking home, they discussed different ideas on how to catch the shape-shifter or try to figure out who it possibly could be.

As they approached the houses, they noticed the front door of the estate was open. They didn't think anything of it and continued up the hill toward the manor. Stephanie was the first to enter and there was Evan sitting on the edge of the desk looking at her. Phineas came in behind her and noticed the way Evan was staring at her, and didn't know what was going on.

"What's wrong," Stephanie asked, walking toward Evan.

"Why did you pull back in shock when I kissed you," Evan said, looking down at the ground then back up at her.

"What do you mean," Stephanie said looking confused.

"About thirty minutes ago, you came up here and asked me a question about Hayden. I went to kiss you and you ran out shocked," Evan said, standing up straight.

"I have no clue what you're talking about. I was with Phineas for the past hour looking up news clips," Stephanie said, pointing to Phineas.

"Yeah we just got back here," Phineas said, walking fully into the den, "I was with her the whole time."

"That's not good then," Evan said, turning around and putting his hands on the desk.

"Why," Phineas asked, walking even further into the room.

"Because I think I must have talked to the shape-shifter," Evan said, looking up over his shoulder.

"That's not a good thing," Phineas said, looking from Evan to Stephanie.

"Yeah, we might want to go check on Hayden's family," Evan said as he stood up and turned to face them.

"Why is that, I am afraid to ask," Phineas said.

"Because, when I thought it was Stephanie, she wanted me to remind her when

Hayden started to change," Evan said, looking at the ground then rubbing the back of his head.

"Ok, so what's so bad about that," Phineas asked, looking up at Evan.

"Well I mentioned that we were told this by Hayden's wife," Evan replied, looking up through squinted eyes.

"Shit, we need to get down there and see if everyone's ok," Phineas said, running towards the door.

"Wait. Stephanie and I will go down there. You stay here and make sure nobody comes after your brother," Evan said, looking between Stephanie and Phineas.

"Ok. Hopefully nothing has happened or I swear, when I get my hands on that shape-shifter...," Phineas said, as he began to walk over to the stairs.

"Don't say anything to Hayden though. We want to make sure before we tell him," Evan said, walking toward Phineas.

"I'm not stupid," Phineas said, and began walking up the stairs.

Evan watched Phineas walk up the stairs and disappear around the corner. He turned to Stephanie and, without saying anything, walked to the door, opened it and walked out on the front porch. Evan closely followed. As they walked slowly down the hill toward the estate, Stephanie could see something was bothering Evan.

"What's wrong," she said, grabbing him by the arm and turning him around.

"If something has happened to Hayden's family, I don't know if I can forgive myself for what I did," Evan said, looking down to the ground.

"You didn't do anything wrong, Evan. This person deceived all of us and apparently, whoever this is, is good at what they're doing," Stephanie said, rubbing Evan's arm.

"Yes, but I know the feeling of losing my family. If something like that happened, I don't think Phineas or Hayden will probably ever talk to me again," Evan said, looking up at her.

"For one, we don't know if anything has happened and two, it's not your fault so stop beating yourself up over this," Stephanie said, grabbing his arm and pulling him down the hill.

As they got closer to the estate, Evan noticed a smell coming from the house. He looked at Stephanie, and she had also noticed the smell. They went running into the house and there, on the floor, was Hayden's wife in a pool of blood. Evan ran over to check her pulse and couldn't find one. Stephanie ran up the stairs and discovered Hayden's children as well, in the same condition as Hayden's wife. They couldn't find Phineas' sister anywhere, and were hoping she got out.

Stephanie stepped outside and tried to control herself from all the blood she had just come upon. She didn't feel the urge to drink it, but felt sick to her stomach from what she had just witnessed. She pulled her cell phone out to make a call up to Phineas while Evan was still inside, searching the house for the person who had did this.

"Hello," Phineas answered rather quickly.

"The shape-shifter got them," she said, waiting for a response.

"All of them, I mean everyone," Phineas asked choked up with sadness.

"Well, we can't find your sister, but Hayden's wife and kids are gone," Stephanie said pausing, "There's something else to."

"What is it," Phineas said, softly.

"Well, Evan is beating himself up over this. He thinks it's his fault," Stephanie said, looking down at the ground.

"It's not his fault. If anyone of us was in his position we would have said the exact same thing," Phineas paused, "Whoever is doing this has tricked us all."

"That's what I told him, but he still isn't convinced," Stephanie said.

"When you guys get back, I will talk to him. For now, you guys watch out down there and I will tell Hayden… somehow," Phineas said.

"Ok, we will be back up there in a bit," Stephanie said, then ended the call.

She walked back in the house to look for Evan when, all of the sudden, there was a scream from the front door. Stephanie looked around and saw Phineas' sister standing in the doorway, about to collapse. She ran over to her and held her up as she began to cry uncontrollably. Evan came running down the stairs and saw Stephanie cradling Jennifer in her arms. He walked up to her and knelt beside her, trying to help calm her.

They slowly got her over to the couch, and Evan cleaned up the body of Hayden's wife, taking her to the other room so Jennifer wouldn't see it. As she slowly calmed down, they decided to ask her where she was.

"Jennifer, I hate to ask, but where were you this afternoon," Evan said, looking at Jennifer with sadness in his eyes.

"I went downtown to meet a friend about a couple of hours ago. When I left everything was ok," she said, looking up at him through teary eyes.

"I think this just happened less than an hour ago, so you were lucky you didn't walk in on it," Evan said, patting her back.

"Oh my god-what about the children," she shrieked, jumping up to go check.

"I wouldn't go up there," Evan said, stepping in front of her.

"Oh no not them too," she said, as she began to cry again. Sobbing she leaned up against Evan, and Evan pulled her in to comfort her. Stephanie came up behind her and rubbed her back to help her calm down.

"I think we need to get her up to the manor," Evan said, looking at Stephanie.

"Wait, we should call the cops," Jennifer said, pulling away from them.

"We can't, we have to do this ourselves," Evan said looking down at her.

"What do you mean? This is a murder! We need to find out who did this so they're caught," she said in a quick pace.

"We already have a good idea who this is and we have to figure this out ourselves," Evan said, backing up a bit.

"No-we need to call the police now," she began to yell.

"We can't," Evan said, getting in her face, "You need to come with us up to the manor so we can explain our reasoning."

They had to pull her out of the house because she didn't want to leave. As they were dragging her up the hill, Phineas came out of the manor and realized they were having difficulty with his sister. He met them half-way down and helped them up to the manor. They sat her down on the sofa in the den and started to explain.

“We didn’t want to tell you down there, but the reason we have to deal with this ourselves is because we are all part of a supernatural event,” Evan said, trying to pick his words carefully.

“I don’t understand,” Jennifer said, looking between the three of them with confusion.

“Lets just say, we are supernatural beings,” Evan said, looking at Phineas and Stephanie.

“I still don’t get what you are talking about,” she said, still looking lost.

“Well, Stephanie and I are vampires, and your brother here is a werewolf,” he said, realizing how crazy it all must sound to her.

“Ok, if you are what you say you are, why the secrecy of not telling the cops,” she said, understanding more.

“The cops would see that it’s the Daniels house and suspect Phineas did it like they thought he killed all those gypsies,” Stephanie answered.

“Wait, do you believe what we told you,” Phineas said, looking down at her in disbelief.

“Yeah, I believe you-mainly because I am,” she paused, looking at the ground and then whispering, “a witch.”

“What? You’re a witch,” Phineas asked, looking shocked, “Wait, black magic or…”

“I never turned you into a toad, did I,” Jennifer said, crossing her arms and raising an eyebrow up to Phineas.

“I guess not,” he said, looking back at her.

“So I guess the Daniels family is cursed,” Jennifer said, this realization helped to calm her in a way, knowing the murders were part of the curse and almost destined to happen.

“What do you mean,” Evan asked.

“Well, I mean I’m a witch, you’re a vampire, he’s a werewolf and Hayden has telekinesis,” she said standing up to join them.

“Hayden is like us too,” Phineas said, completely shocked.

“Yep, ever since he was a kid,” she said, looking at him, “Wait, he didn’t tell you?”

“No, so I am the only one who had to get attacked to get powers,” Phineas said, looking down at the ground.

“Wait, you are forgetting one Daniels that had to get attacked to get his curse as well,” Evan said, raising his hand.

“Oh yeah, I forgot,” Phineas said, looking toward Evan.

“Well, I’m glad we have all these people in our family that can help fight this shape-shifter when we find him or her,” Evan said, looking between the three of them.

“Yeah, we have a family full of freaks and you’re grateful,” Jennifer said, kind of laughing.

“Hey I learned way back that if you don’t accept your gift, you are going to live a miserable life,” Evan said, looking to Jennifer.

“I guess you’re right,” she said, looking back at him.

They all stood in silence not sure what to say to each other. Jennifer decided she wanted to see her brother, and Phineas led her up to his bedroom. Phineas told him about his family. He had a complete mental breakdown. Phineas and Jennifer did their best to calm him.

Evan and Stephanie were waiting downstairs still waiting on news from Melanie. As the sun began to set, Stephanie noticed a person walking up the hill toward the manor. She got close up against the glass and noticed it was her sister carrying cups of something. Stephanie went and opened the door for her as she approached the porch. Melanie came in and sat the cups of hot chocolate on the desk in the den. Evan and Stephanie waited to hear what she had found out.

"So, I found out some very interesting things," she said sitting in a chair across from the two of them.

"What did you find out," Evan asked looking eager.

"Well, you know when you told me that you had seen your brother the day after he was killed," Melanie paused, waiting for Evan to nod, "Well, turns out you were right."

"What do you mean," Evan asked, sitting down in the chair behind the desk.

"Our shape-shifter is none other than… Adam Daniels," Melanie said, with a look of accomplishment on her face.

"You have got to be shitting me," Evan said, leaning back in his desk chair.

Chapter Seventeen

Adam didn't know where exactly he was going. The person he had talked to told him where to find the people he was looking for, but never gave him an exact location.

"This must be their way of detouring people away from finding their lair" Adam thought to himself, looking around the desolate street he was on.

As he began walking further up the street, he noticed an alley with a door at the end of it. He figured this must have been what he was looking for. The pathway to the door was poorly lit, and Adam couldn't see more than a foot in front of him. As he came closer to the door, he noticed the number three above it and knew he was at the right place. He knocked and a pale-faced person answered.

"Can I help you," the man behind the door answered.

"Yes, I'm looking for the leader of the vampires," Adam said, looking behind him to make sure there was no one else listening.

"Who are you and what do you want," the man asked, looking angered.

"I am here to offer information on Evan and Phineas Daniels," Adam said, coming closer to the door.

"Come in, quick," the man said, pulling Adam in.

The hallway that they entered was as dark as the alley. The man continued to pull Adam until they entered into a large room. Adam pulled free and looked around the room. He noticed it looked like a ballroom of some sort. Adam stopped in his tracks as he saw a person sitting at the front of the room in what looked like a throne. The man that had pulled him in was leaning over whispering something into his ear. The man then motioned for Adam to come closer to the person in the throne.

As Adam got closer he noticed the true gothic beauty of the throne itself. The person sitting within the throne was a different matter. The man in the throne was sort of square-faced and cropped hair. Adam couldn't tell which way the person was looking due to the sunglasses that were perched over his eyes.

"My servant says you have information on Evan and Phineas Daniels," the person said, pulling his sunglasses down.

"Yes," Adam said, looking up at the mysterious man.

"How do you know the Daniels," the man asked, looking down at Adam with his dark eyes.

"Well, Evan is my brother and Phineas is my distant cousin," Adam responded, looking down to the ground then back up again.

"So you have come to rat out your own brother," asked the man, looking amused.

"He needs to know where his place is, sir," Adam said with a stern look on his face.

"You are right," the man said pausing to stand up, "He needs to know he can not be friends with a werewolf. I shall go have a meeting with him and discuss his place in the vampire clan."

"He is back in the states on the Daniels property," Adam said, looking up to the very tall man.

"I know where that is, it is rumored to have been the place of the first vampire and werewolf battle," the man said, stepping down from his throne to come eye-to-eye with Adam.

"How was that the location of the first battle, if you don't mind me asking sir," Adam said, looking straight into the dark eyes of the creature that stood before him.

"Well, it was back before it became know as Infirmary Hill," he paused looking from Adam to something cross the room, "I would say back in the early 19th century. That land was suppose to be sacred land to the wolves, but then one of our kind decided to build an infirmary there causing a big uproar. The Infirmary was there to help treat the cursed like ourselves, but the wolves didn't like that. By time they were finished with the place, it was left in rubble. Everybody now knows anything built on that hill curses the people that are associated with it. That's why the Daniels family, your family, is cursed."

"So, we have you to thank for that," Adam said, looking straight ahead.

"No, you have the wolves to thank for that", he paused pulling Adam around, "They are the ones that cursed the land."

"Talking about the wolves, do you know where I can find their leader," Adam asked, hoping not to cause an uproar.

"If you are thinking about turning in your cousin, Phineas, then you are too late. I will be talking to the leader of the wolves to see if he would like to accompany me to talk to the two of them," he said, letting go of Adam's arm.

"Could I come with you when you confront them," Adam said, looking from the floor up toward him.

"Sure," he paused, "we have already sent people to watch over the house until we arrive."

"That's good, we don't want them to pack up and leave," Adam said, following the creature out into the hallway he had walked through.

"But I must ask you to go back to the States now and get the two of them together, out in a wooded area," he said looking at Adam.

“Why in a wooded area,” Adam asked, looking confused.

“Because we don’t want to make a public entrance, if they decide not to come with us,” he said, looking amused by the question.

“How many people will you bring,” asked Adam, with a look of annoyance on his face.

“Well, me and the wolf leader will be alone, other than you,” he paused looking up and down the long corridor, “If they don’t come with us, then they will have to fight us, and I can assure you they won’t win.”

The creature escorted him back to the front door and then left him. As Adam walked back to the silent street, he looked to make sure nobody had seen what alley he had walked out of. Adam walked slowly, enjoying the Canadian air. He then spotted his car and picked up the pace.

He knew he had a job ahead of him, considering he would have to keep them from killing him. How exactly was he going to get them to agree to meet him in a wooded area? He was still uncertain how hw would do it, but he had to think fast because he didn't have much time.

Chapter Eighteen

After Melanie told Evan and Stephanie about Adam, there was silence in the room. Evan looked at Melanie, then back to the desk in shock of what he had just been told. He knew he had seen his brother the day after he supposedly died, but to still be alive over one hundred years, he couldn't wrap his brain around it.

"You never told me you had a brother," Stephanie said, breaking the silence.

"I never thought he would come up," Evan said, looking at the desk shaking his head.

"So what did your guy have to say about this brother of Evan's," Stephanie said, looking over at Evan with a mocking tone.

"Well he said that he thought he was dead because there hasn't been any activity with him since about a hundred years ago," Melanie said, leaning up against the desk.

"So he might still be dead," Evan said perking up.

"Yeah there's a slight chance but who else would be in this location and in the Daniels family home," she said, pausing to turn toward Evan, "I can't think of any better suspect."

"This isn't good," Evan said, standing up from behind the desk, "Why would my brother do this to us or me for that matter? We have always had a good relationship up until the year he died."

"Why? What happened that year," Stephanie asked, getting closer to Melanie and Evan.

"That was the year my parents were going to give me money for school," Evan said, rubbing the back of his neck.

"How's that a problem," Melanie asked.

"Well it shouldn't have been a problem, except four years earlier Adam asked my parents for money to go to school and they didn't have it then. He got so pissed off at me that he swore a personal vendetta against me."

"A personal vendetta," Stephanie chuckled.

"It's not funny-he threatened my life because of this," Evan said, pausing and looking up at Stephanie. "He was mad because, in his eyes, the only reason I was getting the money and not him was because I was the baby of the family and my parents' favorite."

"Oh, the old 'favorite son' routine," Melanie said, with a smirk on her face, "What a classic tale."

"Yeah, that excuse has been around forever, believe me," Evan said, sitting back in the desk chair.

"Sometimes though, I think our parents tried to pit us against each other," Evan said, looking up at the both of them, "Believe me, my parents were no angels."

"Sadly, most parents seem to do that," Melanie said, looking down at the desk.

"So, what are we going to do about Adam, even though he clearly killed those people down there," Stephanie said, looking from Melanie to Evan.

"Did he," Evan asked looking at Stephanie, "I don't think he did."

"Ok, I am sorry your brother is behind all of this, but he was the only one who knew we got the answers from the wife," Stephanie said looking down toward him.

"We need to go down and check out the scene again. I think there is something we have missed," Evan said, looking between the two of them.

"Ok Evan, but I have no clue what you are expecting to find," Stephanie said, reaching for his hand.

"I think I already found it, but I just have to go back and check before I make any conclusions," Evan answered, standing up to take Stephanie's hand.

The three of them walked out the door and headed down the hill toward the estate. As they descended the hill, Melanie knew that Evan was just trying to find another explanation to help clear his brother's name. She knew that they had their history but she believed Evan thought he might be able to salvage their relationship, if Adam was truly alive.

They stopped just outside of the house. Evan pulled Stephanie inside and he began searching, for what, neither Melanie nor

Stephanie knew. Evan went to where he pulled Hayden's wife's body out of the way and began to check the body. He noticed on the neck there were puncture wounds and that was where the blood came from.

"Hey girls, I found it," Evan yelled over his shoulder to Melanie and Stephanie.

"What did you find," Stephanie said coming closer.

"Puncture wounds on the side of the neck. What does that tell you," Evan said, smirking while kneeling beside the body.

"A vampire," Stephanie answered with a gasp.

"Yep," Evan said, looking up at the both of them.

"Yeah, but Evan remember, when who ever shifted into Phineas had his ability to change into a werewolf then who's to say whoever shifted into me wasn't able to shift into a vampire as well," Stephanie said, looking down with compassion.

"She's right Evan. Whoever did this could have been able to shift into a vampire too," Melanie said, touching Evan's shoulder.

"That's true, I guess," Evan said pausing, "We need to see if Adam is alive before we blame him though."

"Yeah, we should do that," Melanie said pausing, "but let's not tell the others until we are sure of who it is."

"Yeah, I don't want them hunting down my brother before I get a hold of him," Evan said, standing up beside the two girls.

"Where is he buried," Melanie said, looking up at Evan.

"In the Daniels crypt," Evan responded.

"In the basement," Stephanie asked.

"No, that's the older relatives," Evan paused looking at Stephanie, "He was the first burial in the new crypt in the old part of the cemetery."

"Well we better go check it out," Melanie said turning around to leave.

They walked out the front door of the estate and headed back up the path to the manor. They walked to the edge of the hill and descended into the grave yard below. Evan couldn't remember exactly where his family crypt was but thought it was somewhere close to the edge of the cemetery by the hill. As they walked around, they kept an eye out for the Daniels name on the grave stones.

Stephanie spotted several old stones that had the name on them, but no crypt. She continued to check out the ground when she ran into a building right in front of her. As she was rubbing her head, she walked around the front of it and written into the grayish-white marble was the name DANIELS.

"Hey guys, I'm not sure, but I think I found it," Stephanie said, looking over her shoulders and still rubbing her head.

"That's it," Evan said looking up at it, "Beautiful, isn't it."

"It is! It has an otherworldly charm about it," Melanie said, as she came up next to Stephanie and Evan.

"What's wrong with you, Stephanie," Evan asked, noticing her rubbing her head.

"Let's just say I didn't find the crypt, my head did," Stephanie said, looking up at Evan with a smile on her face.

"Are you ok," Evan said, unable to keep the smile from his face.

"Yeah, I'll be ok," Stephanie said.

"So, how do we get in here-it's locked," Melanie said, getting closer to inspect the entrance to the crypt.

"This way," Evan said, snapping the lock off with one hand.

"Yep, that will do it," Melanie said, standing back up to look at Evan.

"Now how are we suppose to unearth Adam's casket," Stephanie asked as they all three got inside the crypt.

"It does look like it's going to be a problem with that big cement slab covering his resting place," Melanie said, looking at Stephanie.

Evan found a cast iron candlestick in the corner of the crypt and picked it up. He took it over to the cement slab and hit it into the slab. The girls jumped back, visibly frightened of the sudden loud noise.

"Are you going to keep breaking things like that," Melanie said, trying to shake what just happened.

"Maybe. I have to say it gets my frustrations out," he said with a smirk on his face as he lowered the holder.

"You should do the honors of opening it up. I mean, he is your brother," Stephanie said standing back from the casket.

"Why? Are you scared? Do you think he might be a zombie," Evan said with a chuckle.

"You never know," Melanie answered back, looking just as scared as Stephanie.

"Zombies aren't real, that's just myth," Evan said pulling the casket out.

"So says the vampire," Stephanie said in a mocking tone.

"I guess you have a point there," Evan said, turning around toward them.

Evan turned back around and looked at the coffin. It made all the memories from the past hundred years come back to him. Being locked in a small area was no fun, especially when you couldn't even escape by dying.

He looked back down toward the coffin and got prepared to open the lid. As he pulled the lid open, he jumped when the girls let out a little scream. Doing this made him drop the lid and he had to start all over again. He thought it was better to do it like a band-aid and get it over with. He threw open the coffin and turned his head closing his eyes in the process. There was a low gasp from the girls and Evan knew there must have been something in the coffin.

As he shifted his gaze back around, he noticed the girls wide-eyed and coming closer to the coffin. He turned to look down and there, in the coffin, was what he could only describe as the caretaker of the cemetery.

"That's definitely not Adam," Evan said looking back up towards the girls.

"We kind of already guessed that," Melanie said looking from the coffin to Evan.

"Who is that then, if it's not Adam," Stephanie said holding onto Melanie's arm.

"It looks like an old caretaker of the cemetery," Evan said, pausing to look at Stephanie, "He must have been killed and stuffed in this box back when Adam supposedly died."

"So in reality, he has been alive all this time," Stephanie said walking over to Evan to hold his arm.

"I guess so," Evan said looking into her eyes.

"What now," Melanie asked.

"Does your guy know where Adam might be," Evan asked, looking back at Melanie.

"I am not sure," Melanie said looking at the casket and then back up to him, "He might. Do you want me to contact him?"

"I think that might be the wise idea to do so we can see where this asshole of a brother of mine might be," Evan said, sliding the coffin back into place.

Stephanie, noticing the hurt in Evan's voice, stayed with him the whole walk back. As they were getting toward the top of the hill, Melanie decided to call Lucas to see if he knew anything about Adam's whereabouts. Evan sat on a bench that overlooked the whole cemetery and Stephanie sat beside him. She could see he was hurting inside and she wanted to comfort him.

"What's wrong," she asked, looking up at him with her head on his shoulder.

"It just hurts me, that's all. That my brother would do this kind of thing to me," he answered back to her, looking straight ahead.

"I'm taking it deep down you truly loved and cared about your brother," Stephanie said looking out over the cemetery.

"We were the best of friends, and he was the best brother you could ask for," Evan paused, getting a little teary-eyed, "It was our parents who turned us against each other. I even told them I didn't want the money since Adam didn't go to school, but they insisted that it wouldn't matter. I shouldn't have listened."

Stephanie just cuddled up to Evan and listened to him as he told her all about his brother and their adventures as kids. She could tell it helped him to get things off his chest and, by time he was finished, he was cuddling with her on the bench.

Chapter Nineteen

Melanie had just hung up the phone, turned around and noticed how close Evan and Stephanie were. She was truly happy for the both of them. She then turned toward the house and noticed Phineas and Jennifer walking their way. Melanie was afraid to say anything to them, thinking it might cause a war between them. As they came closer, she motioned for them to come over to the path.

"So what did you find out," Phineas asked, putting his hands in his winter jacket.

"The person behind all of this is Adam Daniels," Melanie said pausing, "He's Evan's brother."

"What," Phineas seemed shocked, "You have to be kidding me! How is he taking this?"

"Not well," Melanie said, looking from Phineas back to Evan, "I think he is more hurt than anything."

"What are we going to do about this," Jennifer chimed in.

"I have called in Lucas, my inside guy, and he is coming," she said looking between the two of them, "He said he is bringing a person who can help track Adam down for us."

"I am taking it Evan will want us not to kill him," Phineas said, looking up at Melanie.

"It's not that I don't want anybody to kill him," Evan said, walking toward the three of them with Stephanie on his heels, "it's just I want to talk with him first."

"That's a bunch of bull! You will probably let him go-you'll let him get away with murder because he's your brother," Jennifer yelled at Evan, "I say me and Phineas go and track him down and kill him now before he hurts us anymore!"

Evan snapped around and took Jennifer by the throat and slammed her into the nearest tree. His face turned and he was about to attack, but before he could, Stephanie ran up beside him and tried to calm him down. When it looked like she was getting nowhere, Phineas came up and tried to pry Evan off of her.

"You do anything to harm my brother and your life will be gone in an instant, do you understand me," Evan hissed at her.

"Evan she won't do anything," Phineas said, trying to pull him off her.

"How can I trust you? How do I know your not just trying to protect her," Evan answered, snapping his head toward Phineas.

"Listen, if she does anything to harm Adam, not only will you want to kill her… I mean, I would never jeopardize our friendship like that," Phineas answered, back looking sincere.

Evan let go of Jennifer's throat and her body slid down the tree. Phineas helped her up and gave her a stern look. After getting up off the ground, Jennifer went walking after Evan.

"Just to let you know, I don't have to listen to my brother. I can wipe you out too," Jennifer said.

"Oh, really," Evan said snapping around, his eyes blackened.

"Ok, since we can't control her, I think we should put her in the family crypt," Phineas said, running up behind Jennifer and grabbing her hands.

"Sounds like a good idea," Melanie said looking at Phineas.

"I don't care-I can still cast spells from in the crypt," Jennifer snapped back.

“Jennifer stop being stupid,” a voice said, coming from the front porch of the house.

“I can’t believe *you* want me to stop. I mean, it was *your* wife and kids his brother killed,” Jennifer said, trying to pull away from Phineas.

“I think Evan and Phineas can handle him and I am sure they will do what is necessary,” Hayden answered walking off the front porch.

“All he is going to do is protect his brother,” Jennifer answered back.

“I have only known Evan for about three days and I know he will do what has to be done-whether that’s kill his brother or question him,” Hayden said looking into Jennifer’s eyes, “I trust him just like a brother myself.”

“Fine, but don’t come crying to me when he lets his brother kill the rest of us,” Jennifer said, finally getting away from Phineas’s grip.

“So… when is your guy coming,” Phineas asked Melanie, shaking off what just happened.

"He should be here anytime."

"Should we go and wait for him in the manor," Phineas asked, pulling down on his winter coat.

"I think that's a wise idea," Melanie answered, noticing how silent everyone else had become.

They all walked back to the house in silence. Phineas looked at Melanie as they led the pack into the house. The two of them realized they had just diverted a big crisis. They all sat down in the den to wait for Lucas. Stephanie sat beside Evan and rested her head against him, hoping to comfort him. Evan noticed this and wrapped his arm around Stephanie and held her closely.

"Thank you," Evan whispered into Stephanie's ear.

"No problem," she said, leaning closer to him.

"When is this guy of yours coming," Phineas said, looking over to Melanie.

"I'm not sure," Melanie answered, turning toward Phineas, "Last time we met he was there in an instant."

"It doesn't look that way now," Phineas said, looking toward the entrance way then back at Melanie.

"Sorry it took so long," a voice said coming from the entrance hall.

"Wow, no way," Phineas said, standing up in disbelief, "You weren't there a minute ago and I didn't hear the door open."

"I'm mysterious like that," Lucas said with a sly grin on his face.

"Where's the other guy you were supposed to bring," Melanie said standing up to meet him.

"He's outside, he'll be in here in a minute or so," Lucas said, going over to the window looking out.

"What is he doing," Stephanie asked, as she and Evan got up to look out the window as well.

"Something about he had to comfort a tree out there because it had recently been abused," Lucas said shrugging his shoulders.

"Is he doing what I *think* he is doing," Phineas said, walking up beside all of them.

"Yep, looks like he is hugging the tree," Evan said in a serious tone.

"What kind of crazy person did you bring with you," Melanie asked, looking from the scene outside back to Lucas.

"He is caught up on making peace with the Earth, but he is also one of the best trackers out there," Lucas said looking down at Melanie.

"Oh crap, here he comes," Phineas said, looking over to the group, "We should probably get away from the window."

Everyone scattered from the window and sat in different locations around the room, trying their best to act normal. The man that they had seen outside walked into the house and glanced around at each of them.

"Hello, my name is Jason," he said, still glancing around at them.

"Hi Jason," Melanie said getting up to shake his hand, "I'm Melanie, this is Phineas, my sister Stephanie, Evan, and that is Hayden."

"Hello," everybody around the room said at once.

"Hi," Jason answered back, becoming more and more comfortable.

"So, how exactly do you track people," Phineas asked, standing up beside Melanie.

"Well I have to listen to the awesomeness of the Earth and then the planet answers me back where a certain person is," he said, as he walked around the room.

"Ok, so should we get started doing this then," Melanie said, looking at Phineas then to Lucas.

"Yeah, let's get this over with," Lucas said, looking back at Jason.

"Hey-calm down and have some gratitude. It will happen when the Earth wants it to happen," Jason said looking around at them.

"Is he high or something," Phineas whispered to Melanie.

"Yeah, high on life," Jason answered back, standing in front of Stephanie and Evan.

"Jason, I don't mean to rush you, but we really need to hurry up and find Adam," Evan said looking at Jason.

"Ok since you asked nicely I will go see what I can find out," he said as he walked out the door again.

As soon as Jason walked out the door everyone hurried up to the window to see what crazy stuff he would do now. They watched as he got on his knees and then leaned down to the ground.

"If he kisses the ground, I'm going to puke," Phineas said.

At the last minute Jason turned his head and put his ear to the ground. It looked as if he was having a conversation with the ground. He had his eyes closed the whole time until the end. His eyes popped open and everyone that was standing around the window acted as if they weren't watching. They heard Jason laugh and then start talking again.

They went back to watching out the window, but were shocked when Jason was gone. His voice was still out there but they couldn't see him. Then his voice disappeared as well. They were all looking at one another when all of a sudden there was a noise from behind them.

"Did you enjoy the show," Jason said with a grin on his face.

"How the… what the," Phineas said, jumping around to face Jason.

"I think what Phineas is trying to say is how did you get from there to here," Evan said, clearing up what his cousin was trying to say.

"The Earth does mysterious things," Jason said, as he walked over to the group.

“Did you find out where Adam is,” Lucas broke in before anyone else could gather their thoughts.

“Yes, and you won’t have to wait long to find him,” Jason said looking at Evan.

“Why is that,” Stephanie asked, looking back at Evan.

“He is on his way up here,” Jason paused as if in a trance, “about thirty minutes out.”

“Why is he on his way up here,” Phineas looked toward Evan.

“I don’t know, but whatever it is it can’t be good,” Evan answered back.

“What do you mean it can’t be good,” Phineas said, following Evan back to his desk.

“Why would someone walk into a lions den,” Evan said, looking up at Phineas then past him toward the girls.

“Shit, you’re right,” Phineas paused to look over his shoulders at the girls, “Do you think he has backup?”

"No, he is coming by himself," Jason chimed in.

"What the hell could he possibly be thinking," Evan asked, looking up at Phineas out of the corner of his eyes.

"I'm not sure, but we have about thirty minutes to find out," Phineas said looking down at the desk.

"I think we should look around the house and see if we can find any clues on what he might want," Evan said, standing up from his desk.

"What do you think we will find," Phineas asked looking at Evan.

"I am not quite sure, but if Adam was living up here until recently he must have some things from his past up here somewhere," he answered back, looking around to the others.

"You have a point," Melanie said, coming closer to Phineas and Evan, "If I was going to leave my family and friends and go into isolation, I would want some personal belongings."

"Ok, why don't we split up and look around for pictures or documents that might suggest why he is coming back here," Evan said as he walked around the desk toward the rest of the group. "Wait, before we go, Hayden-do you remember anything about the day you came up here and got knocked out?"

"Like what, exactly," Hayden asked, standing up and walking toward Evan.

"Like, were you in any certain room when you were knocked out," Evan asked looking up at Hayden.

"I think it was in one of the bedrooms upstairs. I would have to go look and try to remember which one," Hayden said looking back at Evan.

"I would think that room would probably be the room Adam hid out in," Evan said, pausing to look down at the floor, "but still, we should check the whole house just in case."

Everybody split up except for Evan and Stephanie. They were in the den looking around ever nook and cranny, but were coming up with nothing. Stephanie remembered when, just a week prior, her and Evan were in this exact place looking for something else. She knew it was tearing Evan up about his brother, but she didn't know what else she could do to help him.

Evan was pulling open every drawer and cabinet but couldn't find anything. He went to the desk last and started to pull out the drawers and still-nothing. As he was starting to shut the desk, he heard a thud from the bottom of the desk. He looked under it and, under the drawer he just pushed back in, was a red velvet pouch. He grabbed it and opened it up, and there was an old journal with Adam's initials embossed on the cover.

"I think I found something," Evan said as he stood up from the floor.

"What is it," Stephanie asked, coming closer to Evan.

"I'm not sure, but it's Adam's," Evan paused, "Go tell the others to come back down here-I think this is what we've been looking for."

"Ok," Stephanie said as she went sprinting toward the stairs.

Evan opened the journal and was looking over it carefully when a picture fell out. Evan stuck his finger in the page the picture fell out of, and bent over to pick up the picture that had fallen to the floor. He picked it up with his trembling hand and turned it over to see the picture. As he looked closely, he was shocked at what he saw.

He opened up to the page that the picture came from and began reading. As he read, he became more aggravated and threw the book across the room. He hadn't noticed the group coming down the stairs. He quickly got up and walked out of the room.

Stephanie walked over to the journal and found the picture sticking out of it. She handed it over to Phineas. Phineas looked over the journal entry and picture, and discovered why Evan was so upset. He looked up at Stephanie and then to Melanie.

"Um, Stephanie, I think you should go make sure he's ok," Phineas whispered into Stephanie's ear.

"Why? Is something wrong," Stephanie asked looking up at Phineas.

"I'm sure he will tell you," Phineas said walking over to the others.

"What's wrong, Phineas," Hayden asked, looking concerned.

"Well, it seems the vampire that turned Evan was sent by his brother," Phineas paused looking up from the journal in his hand, "I guess they were good friends and Adam asked if he would kill his brother for him."

"That's terrible," Melanie said looking shocked.

"Listen to this," Phineas paused, opening the book then reading, "I have done something terrible, but my cruel brother deserved it. As I write this, he is dead, and I am grateful for it. My parents will soon realize that I was the better child."

"So, he had his own brother murdered," Hayden said, shocked and horrified.

"Wait, it gets better," Phineas paused again, skipping to the end of the journal, "I realized tonight that Evan is not dead. I saw him walking around in the house. I am glad that my friend came back here after my brother tried to kill him. When the morning comes, I am going to let him know he needs to finish the job."

"You mean to tell me he didn't get his brother killed once, but twice, or so he thought," Hayden said getting annoyed.

"Yeah, what a dick," Phineas said closing the book.

"Do you think this will make him want to kill Adam now," Hayden asked quietly.

"I truly don't know," Phineas said looking down at the ground, "It has to be hard on him. I mean, today he finds out his brother is still alive, and now this. He has to be torn up inside."

"I'm so sorry," Stephanie said, comforting Evan for the third time today.

"I just don't know what to do anymore," Evan paused, looking up at Stephanie, "I mean, do I kill him for what he tried to do to me or do I try and get my old brother back?"

"I am not quite sure what to tell you to do. That's something you have to decide on your own," she answered looking over to Evan.

"I guess everyone is entitled to sharing their side of the story," he said looking back toward the kitchen floor.

"True," Stephanie said, taking her gaze off Evan and onto the floor as well.

Evan got up from the bench sitting against the kitchen wall and reached for Stephanie's hand. They walked back into the den and everyone looked toward Evan with sorrow in their eyes. Evan sat on the corner of the desk trying not to make eye contact with anyone other than Stephanie. As the room was quiet, a knock came from the front door. Evan's head snapped up toward the noise and his eyes went solid black. Phineas stood up from his chair and slowly walked towards the door. But in a blink of an eye, Evan was standing in front of him opening the door.

"Hello baby brother," Adam said from the other side of the door.

"Hello to yourself," Evan sneered at Adam.

"Oh what-no love for your older brother," Adam said with a smirk on his face.

"Cut the shit Adam, what do you want," Phineas asked looking from Evan to Adam.

"Evan, that's cute, you have your lap dog as protection," Adam again smirked at Phineas.

"He isn't anybody's lap dog," Evan hissed, back trying not to attack his brother.

"Well while you are both here, I need to see you down in the Moore," Adam said, pointing behind him.

"Fine, we'll go with you," Evan said, looking from Adam to Phineas.

"Good," Adam said, walking off the porch.

"What are we doing," Phineas asked grabbing Evan by the arm.

"We are getting him alone so we can make the kill," Evan said with a grin on his face, and his eyes still black as night.

"Ok, in that case, I'm with you," Phineas said following Evan.

Phineas and Evan grabbed their winter coats and followed Adam out onto the front lawn of the manor. They followed him around the side of the house and down the steep hill that led to the Moore's below. The tension in the air between the three of them was palpable. Phineas began to wonder if they weren't walking into a trap of some kind that Adam had rigged up somewhere out in the woods. Evan also began wondering this after the cold air calmed him down a little.

Chapter Twenty

“The Earth doesn’t feel good about this,” Jason said looking at the girls.

“What do you mean ‘the Earth doesn’t feel god about this’,” Melanie asked, looking worried.

“There’s going to be blood spilt,” Jason said, looking to the floor for answers.

“Then, in that case, we need to get down to the Moore’s and quick,” Stephanie said, looking toward Melanie.

Stephanie grabbed Jason’s hand while Melanie grabbed Lucas’ hand and pulled them through the house. Hayden led the way to the basement door, he pulled the door open and Melanie began to descend the stairs. The group ran through the basement and came to the tunnel entrance. Melanie opened the door to the tunnel and began down the long corridor toward the door leading to the side of the hill. She kept her hand out to feel for the door she would have to go through. Her hand slid over the cold, wet wall until it ran over a metal door. She pushed it open and entered into the short corridor to the hill.

The door on the side of the hill swung open and the five of them walked out onto the hill. As they scanned the woods, they couldn’t see where Adam had taken Phineas and Evan. They descended the hill and entered in to the

Moore and began to listen quietly for clues of where they were.

The farther they got into the Moore the more confusing it was to navigate. Finally Jason leaned down to the ground and felt the vibrations of the Earth. He looked up through the woods and leaned his head out as if trying to hear carefully. After a few seconds he turned and pointed straight ahead, and the group followed. Jason was now leading the group through the woods. He would zigzag through the trees and continued to listen every few steps.

Finally they saw the outline of the three of them in the clearing ahead. They each took separate trees to hide behind. Jason got behind a tree and hugged onto it and squeezed as Stephanie watched in disbelief.

"What are you doing," Stephanie whispered, looking at Jason and trying to pay attention to what was going on in front of the tree.

"I'm giving love to this tree," Jason said, still holding onto the tree.

"One question," Stephanie said, looking from the scene out front to Jason.

"What's that," Jason whispered back.

"You have never been laid before have you," Stephanie said stifling a chuckle.

"I am not sure what you are asking exactly," Jason said, looking baffled.

"Never mind," Stephanie said, looking back to the front of the tree.

As the group stood behind the trees, they didn't notice anything going on. There was no talking or voices coming from the direction of Evan and Phineas. They continued to watch, when all of the sudden, another person appeared in the clearing. Right after that person appeared, another one appeared on the other side of the clearing. Each of these new people looked like they were on a mission. Without thinking, Hayden jumped out from behind the tree and was prepared to attack. The rest of the group saw this and ran after him, but it was too late. The clearing was now full of people as they glanced from one person to the next.

"Who are all of these people, Adam," the tallest figure said.

"I assure you, I didn't invite them," Adam said, stepping back from the group of people.

"We are here to protect Evan and Phineas," Stephanie shot back to the man.

"Stephanie, we got this. You guys take Adam back up to the estate and lock him in the crypt. We will be up in a bit," Evan said, looking over toward them.

"Are you sure," Hayden looked at Evan then to Phineas.

"Yeah, we have this under control," Phineas answered back, looking over at Hayden.

Stephanie ran over to Adam, grabbed him by the arm and disappeared into the night. Melanie, Hayden, Lucas and Jason followed, having to run to catch up. When they finally disappeared into the woods, Evan and Phineas looked back at the two guys that were left with them.

Chapter Twenty-One

"So, who are you and how much has my brother paid you to kill us," Evan asked, looking from the one guy to the other.

"We don't want to kill you, but you need to know that, what you guys are… you can't be friends," the guy nearest Evan said as he walked out of the shadows.

"And why not," Evan asked, looking the guy over.

"Because werewolves and vampires can't be friends, we are mortal enemies," the guy behind them answered.

"Well, I don't like that rule," Phineas said, turning around to where his back was against Evan's back.

"Then, we will kill you if you don't listen to us and split up now," the guy in front of Evan said.

"And who exactly are you again," Evan asked, looking a bit annoyed.

"I am the head of the vampire clan," the man said.

"And I am the head of the werewolf clan," the man in front of Phineas said.

"So what do you decide to do," the vampire asked, looking at Evan.

"I have decided to stand my ground," Evan answered back.

"And your decision Phineas," the werewolf asked.

"Same here," Phineas answered.

“Then, we will have to kill you for betraying your own kind,” the vampire said as he turned. Evan turned and jumped at the vampire.

Phineas transformed into a wolf and leaped toward the werewolf. Evan was thrown up against the tree and almost passed out. He got up and looked at his prey across the clearing. Both of them jumped into the air and began an attack in mid-air. The vampire was choking Evan as the fight came back down to the ground. Evan held his hand behind his back and pulled out the piece of wood he had picked up off the ground and plunged it into the vampire’s chest. The vampire stumbled back and slumped over on the ground. Evan walked over to the vampire and pushed the piece of wood in deeper. Where there was a vampire a few seconds ago, was just a pile of ash now.

Phineas was having tougher luck with his fighting foe. Evan ran over to help Phineas out. As they began their assault, the werewolf came at them at full force. Evan jumped on its back while

Phineas threw his claws into his face. With one twist of the neck, the wolf's spine snapped and killed it instantly. Phineas changed back to his form as did Evan. They brushed themselves off and began to walk back up to the estate where their next project awaited them.

Chapter Twenty-Two

Stephanie got up to the estate first and was still holding on to Adam. She opened up the crypt. It brought back memories of just a few days before when she herself was locked up in that same place. She threw Adam in the crypt with the deer carcasses leftover from before. After she made sure that Adam was secure in the crypt, she slammed the door behind her and locked it. She turned around just as the others were entering the basement.

"Did you have any trouble getting him in there," Melanie asked, coming up to Stephanie.

"Nope, just threw him in and shut the door," Stephanie said as she walked over to the chair against the wall.

"That's a good thing," Melanie said, taking a seat beside Hayden on Phineas' bed.

"I hope Phineas and Evan are ok up there with those guys," Hayden said looking at Melanie.

"I'm sure they'll be ok," Melanie said pausing, watching Stephanie.

"I'm not sure about that. You do know who those guys were, don't you," Lucas said, coming closer and crossing his arms.

"No, who were they," Melanie asked, looking from Hayden to Lucas.

"The one was Nick, the leader of the vampires," Lucas said pausing, running his hand through his hair. “The other was Zack, the leader of the werewolves.”

“That can’t be good,” Hayden said standing up. “Should we go and see if they need any help?”

“What those two were going to do will have already been done. Hopefully Phineas and Evan survived it,” Lucas said as he walked closer to the crypt.

“I need to get some air,” Stephanie said, standing up and walking toward the basement stairs.

“Do you want me to go with you,” Melanie asked looking up at her.

“No, I’ll be fine,” she said as she ascended the stairs.

Melanie and Hayden sat on the bed while Lucas and Jason leaned up against the wall. They were all waiting for something that they thought would never come. But as their fears got the best of them, in through the tunnel came Evan and

Phineas. Both of them looked pretty beat up, but still alive.

Melanie ran up to Phineas and wrapped her arms around him with tears streaming down her face. Lucas, Jason, and Hayden went up to Evan to see what had taken place after they had left.

"So how did you guys beat those two," Lucas asked, looking extremely interested.

"By pure luck, I have to say," Evan said rubbing his forehead.

"I would say those are the strongest of their kind," Lucas said looking between him, Jason and Hayden. "I think we might have a bigger problem on our hands after what you guys did."

"What problem," Evan asked, looking towards Phineas then back to Lucas.

"Well, you two killed the most powerful vampire and werewolf tonight. You don't expect that to go unnoticed, do you," Lucas said, looking serious.

“I didn’t think about that,” Evan said, looking past them. “Wait, where’s Stephanie?”

“She went out to get some air. Do you want me to go get her,” Melanie said, looking over at Evan.

“Yeah, if you don’t mind, that is,” Evan said sitting down on a chair.

Melanie went running up the stairs two at a time to get to Stephanie. As she did, the guys waited in the basement for their return. The silence was broken by Hayden as he stood up and walked toward the crypt.

“What are you going to do with him,” Hayden said looking back at Evan.

“Well, first I am going to talk to him and try not to kill him,” he said, looking up at Hayden.

“Do you think you can trust what he says,” Lucas chimed in.

“I’m not sure if I can trust anything he says, but everybody has a right to be heard,” Evan said standing up.

"Guys, we have a problem," Melanie's voice drifted down the stairs.

"What's that," Phineas asked, standing up and running to the stairs.

"Stephanie is gone-no trace of her whatsoever," Melanie said looking around as she stepped off the last stair.

"Wait-did anybody see her put Adam in the crypt," Evan asked, looking around at all of them.

"No, come to think of it, she was latching the door when we arrived." Melanie said, coming closer to Evan.

Evan ran to the crypt and ripped the lock off the door. The lock fell to the floor with a loud thud and the door popped open. Evan flung the door back and ran inside. As he looked around the room he saw, in the farthest corner, a person shackled to the wall. He ran over and discovered it was Stephanie lying against the wall. He ripped open the shackles and freed her hands. He leaned down and picked her up, carrying her out to the main part of the basement.

The group gathered around and watched to see if she was still alive. No response came from her as she lay on the ground. Evan pulled Melanie over to the side of the basement.

“She needs human blood to be strong again,” Evan said, looking deeply into Melanie’s eyes.

“You want her to drain me,” Melanie asked, looking at Evan in shock.

“No, I just need to cut you and bleed a little bit so she can heal,” Evan said looking over at Stephanie.

“Ok, here… do it fast,” Melanie said, giving Evan her arm.

Evan bit into Melanie’s arm and started to draw blood. He pulled her over to Stephanie and lowered her arm down to her mouth. The blood rolled down Melanie’s arm and entered into her sister’s mouth. Slowly Stephanie’s eyes flickered open and she sat up wiping her mouth with her sleeve. Evan grabbed a hold of her and pulled her into a tight embrace.

"What happened," Stephanie asked, rubbing her head.

"Well, what do you remember about putting Adam into the crypt," Melanie asked, holding onto her arm.

"The last thing I remember was getting ready to shackle Adam up and then something bashed into my skull," she said, looking up at everyone.

"It seems Adam locked you up and changed into you," Evan said, looking from Stephanie to Melanie. "He got away before we got here."

"You have got to be kidding me," Stephanie said trying to stand up.

"Nope, and now he is out there probably plotting new ways of killing us," Phineas said, rubbing the back of his neck.

"I'm sorry guys," Stephanie said, leaning up against Evan.

“No need to be sorry, Steph,” Phineas said looking up at her. “We underestimated his strength.”

“Yeah, he seemed so silent when I got him here,” Stephanie said, looking up at Evan.

“He was probably plotting out what he was going to do,” Evan said looking down at her.

They all sat around not sure what to do. After about an hour of sitting around, unable to come up with any ideas on how to capture Adam, they figured they would just give up until he came to them. But, with that thought, Lucas jumped up and pulled out his cell phone.

“I am going to go make some calls. Maybe other people know his whereabouts,” Lucas said running up the stairs.

Chapter Twenty-Three

Sitting in the back of a black car was a women's silhouette. As the car started to pick up speed, the street lights were cascading in through the windows and lighting up the young lady's face.

Her hair was reddish-brown and a little longer than shoulder length. Her face was kind and gentle, but with a hint of authority in it. As she watched out the window, she saw the blur of water that she was passing over at top speed. She began to look worried, until a distant phone rang in the car. Her head snapped toward the front of the car and watched as the driver spoke. She knew where she was headed and was hoping to be applauded for her work.

The car began to slow down as it entered into a small town. She again started to look out the windows at the buildings as they passed, recognizing the town she was forced to grow up in. They pulled up in front of a mansion that was set back on a hill. As the driver got out, she slid over to the side of the car and waited for it to be opened. It opened up and she slowly stepped out and looked at the Victorian-style mansion she had lived in most of her life.

The front door of the house opened and the driver of the car ushered her up to it. The man at the door grabbed her by the arm and dragged her down the hall to double sliding doors. In the dim light of the house, you could see the lady was wearing a dark skirt and a dark blouse.

They entered into the room and the man dropped her arm. She slowly began to walk to the front of the room where a big oak desk sat with a chair behind it facing the opposite wall. She noticed the moon shone brightly into the office through the big window that was in front of the chair. The women slowly sat down in a chair across from the desk.

"Did you accomplish our goal," a man's deep voice came from the chair.

"Well, I didn't accomplish "*the*" goal," the woman began. "I did lead them to cause a war."

"What do you mean, a war," the man asked, still looking at the opposite wall.

"They killed the vampire and werewolf I got to meet with them," the women said, looking a little terrified.

"You got them to kill the strongest of both our kinds and you think I would be happy," the voice sounded irritated.

"I thought you would be proud, I mean, didn't you always say would wanted to start the war and become the leader of the pack," the women paused. "I figured killing the leader of the werewolf pack would clear the way for you to become the leader."

"I am proud of you honey," the man's voice said as he slowly turned the chair around.

"I knew you would be daddy," the women jumped up and went to hug her father.

"How shall we celebrate your accomplishments," the father said, holding on to his daughter.

"I say we go have a big supper," she said, letting go of her father.

"I say you're a smart girl," the father said, standing up to lead the way out of the study.

Chapter Twenty-Four

The group waited in the basement for Lucas to get back. They sat in silence and occasionally glanced at each other. The silence was broken when the basement door flew open and shut with a bang. Everyone was expecting Lucas, but were surprised to see Jennifer. Jennifer walked down the stairs with anger in her eyes, still not forgiving them for what they were going to do with Adam.

“So where is he,” Jennifer asked as she walked further into the room.

“He’s not here,” Phineas said, looking at her with anger as well. “He knocked out Stephanie and took her shape. After fooling us all he left and we don’t know where he went.”

“I told you we should have killed him while we had the chance,” Jennifer said crossing her arms.

“Yeah, you’re right, it’s all my fault,” Evan said standing up to look the other way.

“What are you trying to do now, get sympathy,” Jennifer barked at Evan.

“You leave him alone,” Hayden said standing up next to Evan. “It’s not his fault he got away. We had him but he overpowered Stephanie, which we didn’t think could happen, so we are all responsible if you really want to point fingers.”

“Well, not me. I *told* you we should go after him and kill him,” Jennifer said with a smug look on her face.

"You know what, Jennifer, you're big talk but no action," Phineas said, standing up by his sister. "I mean, after we said no, you could have went after him all by yourself… but no, it's like you want people to do stuff like that for you!"

"Ok guys, arguing will get us nowhere," Melanie said trying to break it up.

"Yeah, how is this going to help us find Adam," Stephanie said, waving her hand between the two of them.

The room fell silent with tension still thick in the air. As they all went back to sitting down, nobody spoke a word. Evan sat back down by Stephanie and put his arm around her. She leaned into his embrace and looked up into his eyes. The silence broke yet again when the basement door again flung open and shut. Loud thuds came thumping down the stairs and then Lucas appeared at the bottom of them. He walked over to the front of the crypt and paced back in forth thinking of what to say. Everyone followed him back and forth with their eyes.

“Well I have some good news, bad news and worse news-which would you rather hear first,” Lucas said, looking up at them and rubbing his chin.

“Good news first,” Phineas said, looking optimistic.

“The good news is that I know where Adam is,” he said, looking back at all their blank stares.

“And the bad news,” Evan asked, looking from him to the floor bracing for the worst.

“The bad news is he isn’t Adam,” he said looking at the floor.

“We know he’s Stephanie-or at least looked like her when he left here,” said Phineas.

“No, I don’t mean that-he’s not Adam at all. He’s not even a ‘he’,” Lucas blurted out.

Everybody just stared at him with shock on their face. Nobody could believe what he had just told them. Thoughts were racing through Evans head, trying to make some sense out of what he just heard.

“It appears who we thought was Adam was actually April Daniels,” he said pausing, “Adam’s twin sister.”

“So they were both shape-shifters,” Melanie said looking up at Lucas.

“Nope, just her I guess she played Adam so long, that’s why it said Adam was the shape-shifter,” he said, standing with his hands on his hips. “Adam actually did die when it said he did.”

“But wait, that doesn’t explain Adam’s grave and the journal with the picture of Adam and the one vampire,” Evan said, looking up at the whole group. “And I didn’t have a sister.”

“Well, I bet if you find where an April Daniels grave is, Adam’s bones are probably there,” Lucas said, looking at Evan. “And the reason you wouldn’t remember her was because, supposedly, your parents had her sent away after you were just a couple of years old.”

“There’s an April Daniels buried in the family crypt behind you,” Stephanie said, standing up with a look of realization.

“Why don’t we open her grave and give it a look,” Hayden said, standing up and walking towards the crypt.

As Hayden entered, he was quickly followed by Evan and the rest of the group. Evan helped him release the headstone off the front of the burial place. Slowly they pulled the coffin out and laid it on the cement slab that was in the middle of the room. Hayden jerked up on the lid and it popped open, releasing a smell of rotten flesh and bone dust into the air. Evan peered in the coffin and confirmed, by looking at the clothes, that it was his brother Adam. He was sad by this turn of events, hoping to get his brother back, and yet he was dead.

“But what about the journal and the picture,” Evan asked as he looked up to the rest of them.

"I don't know what to say, Evan. I mean, isn't this proof enough." Hayden said looking up at Evan.

"No. I am going to go examine that picture and look at the journal again," Evan said, heading out the door of the crypt and running through the tunnel toward the manor.

The group followed closely behind, trying their best not to fall in the dark corridor. As they came into the basement, they saw Evan already making his way up the stairs toward the main floor. When Evan reached the den, he ripped open the journal and looked at the picture.

He looked closely at the picture and noticed on Adam's left hand, there seemed to be a diamond ring. It looked like a ring that a girl would wear. As he took his time looking slowly over every detail of the picture, he also noticed how the vampire that tried to kill him had his arm wrapped around Adam's waist. It didn't take long to figure it out. He looked up to find the group all circled in the den.

"So, what did you find out," Phineas said, stepping closer to take a look at the picture.

"Look closely at Adam's left hand, and where the vampire's hand is," Evan said, handing Phineas a magnifying glass.

"There's another explanation for this," Phineas said, looking up at Evan.

"I don't believe that there is," Evan said, looking up at Phineas and the rest of the group.

"What are you saying then, Evan," Hayden said, standing closest to the desk.

"I think the vampire that attacked the town and turned me was April's husband, or at least soon-to-be husband," he said, looking down at the journal.

"So, you said something about there being worse news," Evan said, looking from the desk to Lucas.

"Yeah, well you know how you thought you killed your father," Lucas said, waiting for a reply.

“Yes,” Evan answered back, rubbing his eyes.

“Well, he isn’t so dead,” he said, looking at Evan, wincing in anticipation of his reaction.

“And what do you mean by that,” Evan said, looking up at Lucas.

“He was turned into a werewolf about a year after you were born,” Lucas said, stepping closer. “Then when you bit him, he turned into a vampire.”

“So, are you talking about a hybrid creature,” Phineas said, looking at Lucas then back to Evan.

“Yep, pretty much. He is stronger than either race,” Lucas said, looking down at the floor.

“Is my sister and father in this together,” Evan asked, afraid of the answer.

“It appears so,” Lucas paused, coming even closer to the desk. “It seems he wanted the head of the vampires and werewolves killed so he could take the place of both. He also wants to create a war between them."

"Why does he want to do that," Hayden asked, looking more interested with everything Lucas said.

"We think he wants the vampires and werewolves to attack each other and create more hybrids," he said, looking at Hayden

"But whatever happened to the myth about vampires and werewolves dying if they attack each other," Phineas said, looking peeved.

"Well, we know now that's just urban legend because, if that was the case, Evan would have killed his father that night," Lucas said, looking over at Phineas.

"So now we don't have to just worry about Adam, I mean April, we also have to worry about Evan's father," Hayden said, looking up toward Phineas and Evan.

"We are going to have to stop this before it gets out of control," Evan said, standing up straight.

"Where are they now," Phineas asked, turning toward Lucas.

"It seems that they are in Canada, waiting to meet with both clans," Lucas said, looking between the three of them.

"So now we have to come up with a new plan on how to take them down," Evan said, sitting back in the desk chair.

The group took their own seats around the desk, each trying to come up with new ideas on how they were going to stop their new problem. While worrying about the current crisis, they had completely forgotten about their earlier problem. The group was completely silent when a knock came from the door. Jennifer got up and went to answer it, disappearing from the den into the entrance hall.

"Hello officer, please come in," Jennifer's voice said, drifting into the den.

At the mention of an officer, Phineas quickly shot a glance over to Hayden, then to Evan. They all got tense as the officer walked in, holding his hat in his hand, looking around at all of them.

“I’m sorry to bother you but I am here for two reasons,” the officer said, still looking around at the group.

“No bother sir, how may we help you,” Evan said, standing up and offering the officer a seat.

“One reason I am here is I am looking for Detective Nathan. I thought he might be up here,” he said, looking up to Evan.

“I can’t say I have seen him up here tonight,” Evan said, with the group agreeing in unison.

“The other reason is to take your cousin back in for more questioning,” he said, looking over at Phineas.

“Why do they need him for more questioning,” Hayden asked, looking over at the officer.

“I guess they never questioned him in the first place and the detective just took the evidence as enough to find him guilty," the officer said pausing. "But we still need his side of the story so the court has everything they need to look at the case."

"Sorry officer, but there's really no need to do that. I have been meaning to come down to the courthouse to let you know that I have an alibi for Phineas," Jennifer said standing up.

"Oh really, what's his alibi," the officer said, looking interested.

"Well, by time you came to arrest him, I was gone and, like I said, I have been meaning to come down and talk with you about that," Jennifer paused, looking back at Phineas. "That night of the massacre, me and Phineas were down in the basement talking about our childhood memories and catching up with each other. I was with him the whole night I can assure you he never left my sight."

"But how does that explain the driver's license out in the woods," the officer said, looking puzzled.

“I can explain that officer,” Melanie said raising her hand. “Me and Phineas were walking in the woods that afternoon and he was showing me pictures in his wallet. He must have accidently dropped it.”

“That should clear his name then,” the officer said, writing some things down on his notebook. “Um, Mrs….”

“Miss Daniels,” Jennifer said, looking at the officer.

“Miss Daniels, could you come back with me to the precinct so we can get your statement and that should drop the charges against your brother,” the officer said, pausing in his writing. “I, myself, never believed a man could do what I had seen. I still think it was a wild animal, but the detective thought otherwise.”

“Yeah, I can go with you,” Jennifer said, walking closer to the officer.

“Ok, thanks for your time,” the officer said to the rest of the group as he walked out with Jennifer behind.

“So that clears me,” Phineas said, standing up and letting out a long exhale.

“Yeah, but we are still not out of the woods,” Evan said, looking over at Phineas.

“Yeah, I forgot,” Phineas said pausing, “what a buzz kill.”

“I am going to get some air,” Evan said as he walked past the group and out the front door.

Evan stepped out onto the front porch and pulled his winter coat closer around himself as the air became more chilled. He walked down the steps, overlooking the cemetery. Lost in concentration, he hadn’t noticed the rest of the group coming up behind him. Stephanie made him jump as she snuggled up to him, he wrapped his arm around her, holding on tight. Phineas and Melanie did the same on the left side of him. Hayden, Lucas and Jason stood back from the rest of them.

“How are we going to fight off all these creatures,” Stephanie said, looking up at Evan.

“I’m not quite sure yet,” Evan answered back.

“If we can defeat the most powerful vampire and werewolf, we should be able to take on the rest, along with your father and sister,” Phineas said, looking forward.

“I think it might be a little tougher than that Phineas,” Melanie said, looking up at him.

“Whatever the case, you won’t be alone,” Hayden said coming closer.

“We have your backs,” Lucas said, stepping up beside Hayden with Jason following.

“Thanks guys, that means a lot,” Evan said, looking back at them.

“When do we start,” Stephanie asked, looking out over the cemetery.

“I say tomorrow, let’s have tonight for ourselves,” Evan said, looking from Stephanie to out over the cemetery.

Glenn Clay

Is not a typical, normal person, besides being very creative, he is defiantly an original. Not being able to see things as they are, like most people, he usually see things as if there were a story already wrapped around it. Even though he is somewhat of a recluse when he does venture out he is never seen without his trusted wolf ring. *The Cursed and Damned: The Daniels Family* is his first book.

glennclay.wix.com/glennclay

Made in the USA
Charleston, SC
13 May 2013